Southword *46*

Southword is published
by Southword Editions
an imprint of the
Munster Literature Centre
Frank O'Connor House
84 Douglas Street
Cork City T12 X802
Ireland

Issue 46
ISBN 978-1-915573-13-1

www.munsterlit.ie

@MunLitCentre

/southwordjournal

/munsterliteraturecentre

#Southword

Editor
Patrick Cotter

Seán Ó Faoláin International Short Story Competition Judge
Alexander MacLeod

Gregory O'Donoghue International Poetry Competition Judge
Mary O'Donnell

Southword Subscribers' Competitions Judge
James O'Leary

Production
James O'Leary

Thank you to Anne Kennedy for her technical assistance

Cover Image: *'Domestic Madonna'* by Rita Duffy

The Munster Literature Centre is a grateful recipient of funding from

CONTENTS

Poems **70**

Please Subscribe

By subscribing, you will receive new issues of *Southword* straight from the printers, as quickly as we will ourselves. Your subscription will also help to provide us with the resources to make *Southword* even better.

Other perks include access to *Southword Online*, the precursor to the print journal as you know it now. These 26 issues, which appeared on our website from 2009 – 2018, include ten years of writing from our O'Donoghue poetry competition and Ó Faoláin short story competition. You will also have the opportunity to enter our free-to-enter flash fiction competition and poetry competition exclusively for subscribers. Current subscribers are emailed a link every April and may submit up to three poems and/or three pieces of flash fiction; winners are published in our summer issue and receive the following: 1st Prize €150, 2nd prize €100, 3rd prize €75.

Rates for two issues per year:

Ireland, UK, North America, Australia, New Zealand	€24 *postage free*
Rest of Europe	€28 *postage free, tax-inclusive*
Rest of the World	€34 *postage included*

For subscriptions and renewals visit munsterlit.ie.

Southword may also be purchased issue-by-issue through Amazon outlets worldwide and select independent booksellers.

Southword Editor's Poetry Award
Simon Costello

Lord of the Flies

October whistling its rot through the wind chime of the sockets,
this unholy shrine we've raised in the cupboard. How we huddle
and kneel before the severed crown of Moccus,
Ruler of Swine, Celtic Lord of Recovery,
take pliers to his tusks and cast them like dice
across the floor, divine detox from this low god
of last chances.

Kiss the skull, lads, who shed their gills in bowls below the pricks
of brief men, phantoms on the last Stena Line to Holyhead,
who crawled to land like ancient fish
still soaked in the embryonic stain
of deadbeat, sons of fatherhood dumped like tadpoles in a sock
or spat out to be future elegies gummed
beneath the empty chair of a~~n~~ NA meeting. Lads who lay awake
on their Ma's tit listening to rats exist like loose bolts in the attic
or the keys of a dead owner returning
to find renters he never knew
in his lifetime.

Lifetimes of standing in streets, catching rain in their bellies, ignoring
the unstoppable smell of autumn in their mothers, crying tears
like calories. Lifetimes in barns nailing step-Das like heretics
to the walls. Lifetimes of naggins nicked from Dunne's,
of noses punched, leaking, red Rorschachs down shirts,
of school desk graffiti carved into arms and loyalty a butterfly knife
closing its blades like the wings
of a pellet-torn swallow,
a lifetime of birds strewn
like shards of turf across a field.

Fields of lads making blood pacts to the urban myth of Cernunnos,
Kking of cow tipping, Green Man of binge. Fields
where teens met like crows, shared their tongues like regurgitated pellets,
felt the birth of acid in their palms, doomed
to inherit the same grip needed to choke a lover
or hoist a friend up over a gate. Fields
where bales of hay were set alight
and blew the gut skywards off a bull. The clouds of summer '08
unravelling like bowels over
an estate of unfinished homes.

Homes abandoned for uni degrees or trades where fingers vanished
into lime like E dropped in a can. Pay packets dumped like new-borns
at the steps of a bottle of Jäger. Homemade pals dancing down lanes
as night's jaw ground out into diamonds.
Home birds leaving college, flying back to old bedrooms,
going shop to shop with CVs like Jehovahs,
waving off homesick pals boarding planes for the mines of Perth,
emerging home years later
with pockets of Melbas, still half-jarred
and doped up on Xanax.

Xanax-doped lads collecting Job Seekers each Wednesday, flashing their teeth
in the post office to prove they'd no gold in them, whose only decorations
were the altars in their HAP bedsits, posters of Hendrix, Morrison, and Cobain
so far from that greenhouse in Seattle, the 27 Club
rendered in lung yellow.
Xanax-sad lads taking shrooms that never knocked
before entering the hall behind the eyes
but always shut the door behind them. Drank alone
'til every constellation became a sunrise,
'til every day a bedsheet pinned
across a shattered window.

Windows of House Moccus! Ruined Sanctuary of Nosebleeds!
Church of the OD'd! Of shattered lads who sought the self
beneath a bench press, stuffed roids in their chests
'til hearts became the crow trapped
in a boarded-up bedroom, of lads

who roached smack when veins were as rare
as apparitions at Knock, jumped through the stained glass
of the mind in search of missing children. Found only gravity
in the nose-dive down
into their own personal wicker men.

Wicker men, questioned in Garda stations, quiet
as the tequila worm paused in its coffin of amber,
their wicker pal's income a spoon of tar sewn inside an arm. Whose goodbye
was never a *See ya pal* text from Shannon but the sawn-off
misfiring into the wall like starlings twisting over Spain.
Wicker men, burning up like meteors, like jet engines, like manifestos
thrown from a tower. Holding each other
when vipers fell like acid from the sky, sucking venom straight
from the aorta, pissing on a straw brother's ignited legs,
quenching the hallucination of Ouroborous, how he devours his own tail
and is scorched by its answer.

Answer them Moccus! Shaman of Skags, Witchdoctor of Hurt Men
who kept your appointment. Who tired of Russian roulette
with five in the chamber, trekked off-trail in the hard winter of their lives,
grew sick of nights like lost explorers at a fire,
marrow shining beneath jackets, mouths watering
at the answers in each other's meat.
Woke to cow-headed surgeons pressing bolts
like needles between their eyes,
put their udders down their throats
and asked why they couldn't sing.

Pray, Dead Moccus! Pray for those whose brains were snow globes
dropped down a stairs, were scooped into hourglasses
or urns. Pray for those who sang at the doors of Merchant's Quay
with heads like vials of Librium. Sing to those who returned, the last druid
at the treeline of their family, their faces lit up with the horizon
of Midsummer. Oh, Terrible, Moccus! Sing your last hymn
to those who should forget the scent of your breath heavy
with bonfire and forgiveness, you,
the skull turning in the wardrobe, the song heard
behind every ruined lad's door.

Roadkill in Offaly

There's a badger hanging in the basement
purple on its rope. Purple man burrowing
through the kitchen floor drinking gin
with breakfast to balance it out.

A badger will die in its sett over winter,
be dug up by another in spring.
Take enough drugs in the morning
headlights appear like eyes inside a hood.

Truth is no one sees a badger in Tullamore,
like all conservation
it's never about the eating. *Go back,*
I think we hit something.

The truck bumper smacks days from the mouth.
A tyre carves a valley of U through its belly;
tomorrow, a pedestrian will pour a jug of milk
in the tread. With the right dose of speed

a badger spills last year's weather from its neck
at the crossroads. I don't want to dream
in black & white anymore. Like roadkill taken home
I've never felt more emptied.

Stepping Out From the Party for a Moment Is Like Re-watching The Sixth Sense

Out back, it's starlight for miles. The treeline
arrives with supernatural gifts between its fingers:

twigs crushed beneath a boot, the possibility
of an owl. You light a cigarette and it tastes

how it looks in a film. Summer falls from the sky
like stardust on your teeth. For a moment,

it feels good to forget you're nothing,
that someday you won't die in your sleep,

that even though the brain is no one,
it's grown a soft spot for you, like a director

praising their child actor behind the camera
it's been trying its best not to yell cut.

Someone's turned the music back up,
night's throat full of ash, the midges were never

doves full of cream, just cheap bottles of red
wine off your head, shattering in your ear

'til it sounds like your neighbour's lies,
that he hasn't been siphoning diesel

off you for years. Fuck the moon's little flags.
They were never romantic. Six sailors marooned

on an island drinking piss, 'til it tastes like honey
or existence. Down here, you're a pervert looking

through the curtain of your life: 4 a.m.
someone's gone upstairs to call Samaritans,

the table looks like a script with too many lines
of dialogue. A lad chops up a fifty-bag

while his Da finds a pair of boxing gloves.
Is promising everyone he'll go easy on them,

even though you know what happens next,
how tomorrow comes to an end.

1st Prize, Gregory O'Donoghue International Poetry Competition

BEFORE I STILLBIRTHED THE BIRCH

Katie Griffiths

I was great with tree
and thought myself a branchline,
everything connected.

Do you want to know?
I peered at the scan,
perfect besom of tickling twigs.

A bog birch, I suggested.
A ghost birch, said the doctor with huge eyes.
Tree of inference, tree of surmise –

first birch of my lineage,
its nursery prepared,
its earth turned.

But when my stomach grew misshapen
from the butting of boughs
on a wind-raged night

I was alarmed,
the birch unfurling
in a behindhand ambulance

where my hips moved
and I was delivered of tree.
The birth credible

for a moment.
Tiny translucence,
the frondlets I curl around.

Before I stillbirthed the birch
and the mess – bloodied,
greened, flushed –

there'd been the ash,
nearly full-term,
and the hawthorn, lacerating my insides.

But this time, *a ghost birch,*
that would've caught
the darkness off guard.

I drain a water glass.
This is the catalogue of it all.
This is the uphill of it all.

My branchless gaze.
My birchless morning.
My barkless belly, pinched.

2nd Prize, Gregory O'Donoghue International Poetry Competition

AT THE FEET OF MICHELANGELO'S *DAVID*

Suzanne Cleary

They are not the first couple to stand at the feet of *David*
and kiss as if they are saying goodbye at a train station

with one suitcase set between them and the conductor
leaning out his window, bringing the whistle

to his mouth but not yet blowing it,
pressing the cool metal to his lower lip as he watches

travelers rush past the couple as water rushes
around a stone in a river, oh, like attention itself:

a tumbling, ungovernable thing for all but the geniuses
among us, who somehow can concentrate on something

the tour guide is saying about Michelangelo's study of cadavers.
She wants us to look at David's right hand, which hangs

by his side, slightly oversize, its bulging veins proving
that this is the hand of a living man, pulsing with blood.

It is warm and pliant as the hands of this couple
who stand at the feet of the masterpiece,

who are not the first couple to kiss here, but are the last
for today, for the *Accademia* closes in ten minutes. People

press past to buy postcards, posters, tote bags, to reclaim
their umbrellas, for today in Florence

it is pouring wide angel-wings of rain,
which drips onto the tile floor from the hair

of the couple, from the hems of their coats.
They have come here to get out of the rain.

They kiss at the feet of David because he stands
in the gallery off the lobby, and why should they wait?

What better way to make use of their time, so close
to marble made flesh, to the vast head tilted downward, watching?

3rd Prize, Gregory O'Donoghue International Poetry Competition

Sunrise on the Dahme

Zoë Green

Your rowers kiss the river / their blades flashing
black, yellow, red / in the sparkle of the day
– like they're buffing / the scales of a snake
bathing in the sun // tranquil activity

swimmers wringing clothes / a dog jumping
for a ball in the river / as if the river
is his beloved master / a vet back from war.
Seurat would paint him / the boy on the shore

the mother biting an apple // the radio tower
gazes down – forget / the horror, his role –
his mouth of gold teeth / he's harmless now
I used to dread these woods / *with their burial pits*

they still dig up the bones / *the Russians shot*
into the trees until / *no cover remained*
anywhere. Now though / everything is softening,
forgiving to a green pall / this happened (that is all)

today my lover has brought / to our cove his friend
a man in his hammock / shivering, picking
the skin from his hands. / *I am terrified. I lie awake*
from three, paralyzed. / Afraid of what? *Emails.*

Overwhelm. He is stuck / underground with the bones
I have lived there too / there were days I slept through
because that was nothing / and nothing was better
than everything else // but I am learning to be a river

serpent preening in the sun / stretching beneath
rowers' blades, lazing / towards Alt-Schmökwitz
to see what's going down / I do not know where
my lover has gone – only / that one of us has to leave.

The heron opens her chest / to the sun, her wings
hung like panniers / a lady's farthingale
I would have you see / this bird obelisking
at the heat, how hearts / inhale the same blue.

The Killing Centipedes

Dmitry Blizniuk

O Lord, take away immortality,
but leave this cold apple cellar.
Take the souls and all your playthings, but spare our lives,
neither Adam's, nor Eve's, nor your son's,
but my son's life.
This wet cave in the cellar with a wooden floor
is the Promised Land,
but no, we need concrete instead.
The smell of cats, mattresses, a heap of soiled blankets.
The city is alive, but someone sticks shells in it
like needles. A crazy tailor is making
an ugly sleeveless, headless jacket.
But we are people down here,
not mannequins.

The future is a door made of dim plexiglass
the color of unpolished diamonds.
It slides away from you, smoothly, every minute,
with every breath, in or out.
Sometimes faster, sometimes slower if it's curious,
but only in times of peace. In wartime,
the future just jumps away, like a frog or grasshopper.
A moment – and there's nothing ahead,
only a precipice. The void made of
spiteful rectangular pixels
from the game of a maniac
is waltzing.

In times of peace, the epoch slowly, evenly
licks us off,
like ice cream. But now the Kremlin Vova,
the crazy monitor lizard,
gnaws at us, at our blood-soaked earth
strewn with crushed concrete and stone,
his fangs dripping toxic saliva.
The rocket ball of death.

It's hunt for people;
a silver fox breaks the crust of ice over the snow,
diving head first for a vole,
diving for my neighbor Valentina.
Russian murderers are lit with
the shimmering slime of their sick ideas,
and I can see them for tens or hundreds of miles.

Our thoughts bounce like rocks from thick ice.
Our breath turns into white sea weeds.
We hold hands.
The emptiness is black and blue, the night is hungry.
An enormous cougar smells the balconies,
the whites of its eyes shining. Is there anyone alive?
The walls have been uprooted,
the trees have been twisted into a corkscrew.
The broken off staircases lead nowhere like unfinished poems.
The body on the asphalt is not human;
it's just a black and red sleeping bag.
The darkness jumps,
the beast of roar and dust.
There's no place for you and me in this world
of total death.
But you can't drown a sea in blood,
the sea of free people.
The killing centipedes crawling on their mechanical knees
will never grab this land.

Translated by Sergey Gerasimov from Russian

Господи забери бессмертие оставь нам
холодный погреб для яблок.
забери
души. все свои игрушки. только оставь нас в живых.
неАдама неЕву и не твоего - моего
маленького сына.
сырая пещера в подвале с дощатым полом.
земля обетованная.
но нам нужен бетон.
запах кошек матрацы куча засаленных одеял.
а город живой и в него втыкают
снаряды как иглы. безумный портной шьет
уродливую безрукавку безголовку.
но здесь люди.
не манекены.

будущее - дверь из мутно белого оргстекла
цвета неотшлифованных алмазов.
дверь плавно отодвигается от тебя каждую минуту.
каждый вдох выдох.
иногда быстрей иногда медленней если ей любопытно.
это в мирное время. но во время войны
будущее просто отпрыгивает в сторону
как кузнечик или лягушка.
секунда и больше нет ничего впереди
пропасть. пульсирует пустота
сбитая из ехидных квадратиков-пикселей
в игре маньяка.

в мирное время эпоха размеренно медленно
слизывает нас
точно мороженое а сейчас
кремлевский вован сумасшедший варан
грызет нас.
нашу землю пропитанную кровью.
усыпанную кусками бетона щебня.
истекает ядовитой слюной.
ракетный бал смерти.
так чернобурка пробивает снежный наст в прыжке

ныряет в снег
чтобы схватить полевку. соседку валю.
идет охота на людей.
российские убийцы подсвечены
мерцающей слизью больных идей.
я их вижу за десятки сотни километров.

мысли прыгают будто камни по толстому льду.
дыхание превращается в белые водоросли.
держимся за руки.
черно-синяя пустота голодная ночь
исполинская пума обнюхивает балконы.
блестят белки глаз. есть кто живой?
вырваны с корнями стены.
деревья скручены по спирали.
оборванные каменные лестницы как недописаные поэмы.
тело на асфальте - черно-красный спальный мешок:
разве это человек?
тьма прыгнула на.
зверь шума и пыли.
в этом мире тотальной смерти
нет любви сострадания добра. нет места
для тебя и меня.
но не утопить в крови
море море свободных людей.
сороконожкам убийц на механических коленях
не забрать нашу землю.

An uncertain future

Jack Cooper

We'd risk the narrow path to shore when two full moons were to the south,
sneaking through the ruined promenade by their light:
the Moon a freshly minted dime,
the Fuel Moon a penny with green patina.

We'd kiss with sea spray on our lips
while our commune slept in the clifftop bunkhouse
and be in the fields by dawn, the other boys suspecting nothing.

The next night we'd lie restless with longing,
rows of beds between us, listening to the low rumble of freighters
carrying the Fuel Moon's harvest to Earth.

Emptied of its algae, the Fuel Moon is only water and glass:
a patch of rippling starlight.

Our love was something no one else could see.

We passed in the schoolyard without a second glance,
threshed the commune's grain in silence,
kissed girls in the shadows of half-empty silos.

We went into manhood together,
arms waxing from slender crescents to sculpted muscle,
body hair coming in a choking bloom.

It was a night like any other when we were discovered.
We were mortise and tenon on the sand.

The Bering Sea was still as sugar glass,
held in the balance of two tides.

Postscript

Mel Elberger

The ark awaited me and I was instructed to bring the two of what I was:
male of my first name; female of my last. And if I brought them into the ark,
they would survive a deluge fated to obliterate earth's allies, traitors,
dissemblers; even the gratitude of animals. I was permitted to carry in a bag
of feathers and small suitcase of rags; and was told that after the cataclysm,
I would be decreed to release a dove born of my names into a sky of forgiveness.
After the floods subsided, I released the dove, but did not expect
the swift arc of a return. But when it glided back the next day, I did not see
the chip of a shell or maimed seed in its beak, but witnessed the dove alight
on the ark's fractured beam, where the shrewd, darting eyes were the first
to behold the broken world. She returned the following day with a torn blade
of grass in her beak, and I watched if the eyes would sadden, the wings open
to an inner wind. With nothing else but to console the two worlds of
keeping and letting go, the dove held more tightly the fragment retrieved
from all that was abandoned, destroyed; and I heard in a voice humble,
weary and unsure, the trill of an incantation to a new world; wise in praising
the devastation earth could no longer sustain, blessing the ruins by singing.

The Orange

Viviana Fiorentino

a Ghazal for my mother

The night my grandmother died my mum peeled the zest of an orange,
3 a.m. in the dim kitchen light with a knife she cut the zest of an orange.

She gently tore off the pith of the fruit, bent like a craftsman over her table,
stood at the door I caught a glimpse of the white chest of an orange.

A luminous lining, piece by piece I heard the sound of its detachment,
the papery membrane departing the juicy nest of an orange.

In the glow of the lamp light, thousands of aromatic droplets swelled
and expanded in the air, a moment grafted in tears and the breast of an orange.

A sour aromatic smell mixed with the smell of the fish she cooked for dinner,
I came close to her, my sixteen mixed with her forty-nine in the clefts of an orange.

A scrap where I'm not yet born and she's not yet come to light,
both of us dormant and protected, enclosed in the shell, compressed in an orange.

We divided the fruit, quenched our thirst, my name a whisper of her voice,
the juice slid down our warm throats, liquid, fleshed orange.

The Minotaur's Sister

Joanna Grant

I wanted to love him, I really did.
Mother said I should as she pulled
back the wool blanket to show
the black fur, the horn buds, the tiny teeth.

They didn't hurt at first, even when
he'd clamp down on my finger,
my wrist. The first time he drew blood
with those sharpening fangs,
Mother wouldn't look me in the eye
when I complained, my own eyes stung
with tears. *You must have done it,* she'd said.
You angered him. You hurt him first.
Your fault. Not his. Oh, you bad, bad clumsy girl.

I wanted to love him. I tried teaching
him speech, the names of things, like
meat or *bed* or *sleep.* None of them took.
And then in the corners and passages
the headless mice, the wingless birds,
insides ripped out in one long smear.

I tried, but it was never enough. There
Would never, ever, be enough to sate
that black maw, those grunts, those shrieks.
And then, one day, it came, we knew it would—
The bloodstain on the baby's blanket,
the tiny body tossed aside, a broken doll.

When they locked him in the dark,
he cried. As did I. And then I climbed
to the house's flat roof and for the first time
in what seemed like years I sat, back to
the door. Watchful no more. And I wept,
and I wondered, how many other houses,
how many homes with their lamps twinkling

like so many tiny stars, how many of them
hid their own secret trap doors, their heavy bolts,
their wire grilles hot with their heavy secret reek.

The Loaded Gun in Translation

Rosa Lane

After Emily Dickinson's
"My Life had stood a — Loaded Gun —" (754)

I'm ceded — I've stopped being Theirs —
– Emily Dickinson, from 508

I knew the loaded gun // stood / for the non-
belonging // When ten / I studied weapons

of medieval war // carved in a shed /
lit by oil // One thing /

certain / my knife was urgent // whittling
the precise eye / along the grain /

smoothed by grit / the silken edge
of a dagger / battle-ready /

my sword / its decorative pommel / the grip
wrapped with a tongue

from an old boot // the cruciform
hilt // blade hewn to fatal point

swaggering my hip // crossbow and arrows
slung my back // You see / I loved

the butcher's daughter // but she married / the boy
with my cousin's name // who knew

he was the boy / I wanted / to be //
I made three cases full //

buried them / hatches / hinged
flush / with the woods'

soil // Please know / it is not
so much / I did this //

but the unquestionable
necessity of it / the child's battle

cry in the woods / fearless /
valiant / her young dissent

her willingness to die / for the rebel to live

The Horses

Eithne Lannon

of Hollow Bay
are bathing their polished hooves in water,

they move like golden caveats
through ocean's pulled edges,

their velvet nostrils
soft-touch the yellowing air,

their whiskers, thinly dark and pointed
can reach beyond time's timid doorway,

these mythical creatures whose animal minds
can find the human unreachable,

whose large intelligent eyes
see through mine.

Their muscle-layered flanks tremble
to the rider's touch,

their heads rise
and bow into the reins,

their manes are wild
and luscious wind-sheets,

neck veins suspended
with unbridled energy, raised

and knuckled knees exploding
through shallow spittle waves.

O beautiful creatures,
o blessed flesh-spirits,

o lonely wide-eyed seekers.

Dancing Classes in the Nursing Home

Maeve McKenna

December's cold moon has Imelda wild with dancing,
cha-cha-cha-ing down corridors, whistling *Jingle Bells*,
her gown flung wide to reveal leopard skin
panties. Such boldness for a woman her age!
Knuckles pounding doors, she spits at nurses, jives
past, calls out to her mother —*'that fucking bitch'*.

It's 2a.m. or 2p.m., hard to know which.
Imelda and I sway to Eartha Kitt, the dancing
of her fingers on my hips as we jive,
my father two doors down, a miniature Christmas
tree on his windowsill as he ages
from the father I once knew, his blotchy skin

cold as marble; a scarlet tapestry of bruising akin
to my mother's cellulitis leg, that fucking bitch
who left us suddenly one New Year's Eve, ageless
as only a mother's love allows. Imelda is dancing.
She's my mother, she insists, and for Christmas
she promises me a baby, like the one under her pillow, but alive.

At night I half-close the door, slippers glide as Imelda jives
into the room — my father's tongue yellow as his skin —
announcing she wants a Kaftan for Christmas,
swings me round, wild eyed, that facial Diazepam twitch.
She waltzes out, spots her chance, dancing
to the open lift door, fast for her age.

Wheeling a blood pressure monitor, a nurse about my age
sends it rolling across Imelda's path, a hive
of wires wrap around her feet, her hop-scotch dancing.
The lift door slides closed, my dad's motley skin,
roof of his mouth black as the mongrel bitch
pup carried in the palm of his hand for my fifth Christmas.

Will my father live on never to see another Christmas?
We've been at his bedside for ten years, how he stopped aging,
reborn the only son of his adored mother, that bitch
he named her later; cancerous tongue, loving then snide.
'Where is she?', his cries in those early days, retracted skin
under his grey nails, Imelda in a green paper hat, dancing

to *Lonely this Christmas.* Her hand finds mine, dancing
cheek to cheek, the stitch of her nightgown, warmth of her skin,
my father's blue feet, our red hot jive.

Warsaw-Kraków-Białystok

Gloria Sanders

Traversing kilometres we sleep. Dreams
of secret doorways in walls by our feet.
We are watched over. Throw bags underfoot and overhead.
Switch our focus to growing gardens. Follow traces.
We nudge our thoughts to them, to them, to them.

Our need to know the corners they took,
the grass they trod, the music they heard.
We inch towards them. Take ourselves
away. We travel, listen, poke understanding,
or, in the attempt we travel in triangles.

Desecrated outsides drained of colour,
inside, full blooming half daubed language tugs us close to –
We stand when someone says, 'You're in my seat'.
We stand like that a lot. Edging sepia memories,
we retrace forests with our eyes, fingers brush off leaves

dislodge pebbles we did not mean to disturb.
We mean to learn; motives, dates that the
great-great-greats must have chanced
across this market and, before the century turned,
hauled eggs to a new home.

And all this happened before.
In fact (though poetry's no place for facts)
what was before is why we walk.
West to East this time, and this *before*
ripples through once invisible kingdoms.

Land that must have shimmered with transparence.
Fed by red rivers these trees must still have breathed,
our bedfellow worms must still have wriggled, before.
When it was all unknown, we roamed here and there.
Before place-names had edges and outskirts made of stone.

Slicing through mud and air, we expect to be shaken by discovery,
language filling cracks. Our tongues creak in new configurations,
to emphasise an unexpected syllable. We try to glimpse
our great-great-greats greeting each other.

Turning over hundreds of years on our ticket
we shift it from pocket to pocket.

In the Jaffa flea market,

David Allen Sullivan

back in the 70's, I saw—calloused hands I keep
seeing—a hand extend from a salesman
shadowed by suits he was selling, embraced
by the other's responding hand, and the Palestinian
pulled in the Israeli, who leaned into the upright grave
of a sidewalk shop, leaned deep in, beyond vision,
to press cheek to cheek. And night hung in racks
of charcoal and black threads, each empty suit
witness to the way one old man's body greeted
another old man's body—the way kippa
tipped towards keffiyeh. When they parted
those hands lifted up as air rippled in
goodbyes I couldn't hear—then the waters
closed over their encounter. But it's here, rising
up stuttering from memory's coffin, lifting me up
on this day of shelling and shouting and fleeing.
Today I re-hear palm smack palm, feel flesh speak.

Mystic Master Salvador

Tom Harvey

1st Prize, Seán Ó Faoláin International Short Story Competition

---

That summer at Pickering's, past the Clark's Shoes stand and next to the Star Wars figures, there were two blokes who did magic. Beard Guy and his polished head, did disappearing stuff with handkerchiefs. The handkerchiefs didn't disappear, he shoved them in his secret pockets, and Terry Osborn said once, the magic dove escaped and flew round the store, shitting on the nightdresses, 'till the janitor shooed it out a window.

The mums and little kids liked Beard Guy, they'd '*ooo*' and '*ahh*' and clap their stupid hands every time a handkerchief disappeared. We used to go along and take the piss. My dad said, in the Navy *"You give it – or you get it."* It was my fourth school in two years, so I was the one to give it. *'It's up his sleeve,'* or *'it's in his pocket, we can see it.' 'Where's your dove now baldy?'* The mums would shake their heads, like we'd told their precious kids, Father Christmas was just a dad dressed up. Beard Guy would sweat and we'd laugh, and that was the fun. He lasted two weeks.

Saturday, we're expecting Beard Guy, our piss-taking locked and loaded. But it's not him. Instead, a tall bloke with a black moustache and a cloak, comes through the curtains at the back. He walks forward, a magic gunslinger. He stands on the little stage watching us, like he's a king. We're all silent. He looks at us, kind of into us. Suddenly we're all shouting – a black rat has crawled up onto his shoulder, it sits there, he stands there, an eyebrow raised, like it's the most normal thing in the world to have a massive black rat on your shoulder. He lifts a hand for quiet.

'Meet Hades,' he says to us all. 'Hades, meet the children.'

Saturdays at Pickering's changed forever. The man was Mystic Master Salvador, and he was a real magician.

He gets out a pack of cards and I nearly get to be the card picker kid, but Phil Oakley beats me to it. Phil picks a card and shows it just to us, an eight of diamonds. Phil puts it back in the pack. Mystic Master Salvador takes a card from behind Phil's ear, it'll be the eight of diamonds, not bad. He watches us, then, with the eyebrow raise thing, he slowly turns the card round. It's the three of clubs. What's that about? Normally he'd be booed off the stage for messing up the trick, but he has this look of power so we're silent. He puts the three of clubs in Phil's shirt pocket, puts his hand on Phil's shoulder and gives him the *'you will obey me'* look. He stands back up on the stage, all black cloak and magic and tells Phil to take a look. Phil takes the card out of his pocket, the very same card, but it's not the three of clubs it's changed back to the eight of diamonds, which Mystic Master Salvador never even saw. He gets a big shout from us all for that one.

Next, he gets a kid to do a drawing on his magic note pad, he doesn't look at it, but he knows it's a house or a cat or whatever. He makes the house or the cat vanish off the pad and reappear in someone's pocket or bag, and once from down Griff Jenkins' trousers, now that was funny. Things kept appearing in Griff's trousers after that, golf balls, tennis balls and once a Barbie Doll. It gets so Mystic Master Salvador just looks at Griff's trousers and gets a laugh. Griff stopped coming on a Saturday, but we still shout *'what's in yer trousers Griff?'* every time we see him.

Just when you think you know what'll happen next, Mystic Master Salvador does the opposite. He knows the thoughts you have and the thoughts you don't know you have. He knows what you want before you do. *That's* his magic.

We love the stuff he does with Hades. We start the chant, the girls clap and the boys stamp. *'What do we want? HADES! When do we want him? NOW!'* Mystic Master Salvador raises his hand for silence, gives us all a teacher look, like we've done something bad, but the eyebrow raise is his sign that we haven't and it's all ok. Two little black eyes appear on Mystic Master Salvador's shoulder, and we all cheer like we're six again. He always does the intro *'Hades, meet the children.'* Once he made Hades appear in Alison Parker's duffel bag, she screamed, we loved that. Then he'd throw Hades into the air and Hades would vanish. That was good – but there was a trick he did with Hades that beat the others, hands down. None of us knew how he did it. He had this massive old book of magic spells, he'd pretend it had all the names and ages of all the children in all the world. He'd fix one of us with his magic eyes, then look whoever it was up in his book and tell that kid how old he was. It could have been a guess but he was spot on every time. Turns out that wasn't the actual trick. You thought it was but it wasn't. He lets Hades run along the pages, then Hades sits still in the middle of the big book of names. Mystic Master Salvador stares at us with his giant magic eyes. We are so still. Quicker than you can see, he slams the book shut on poor old Hades, fur flies up in the air, the girls scream, we're gutted he'd kill his own rat, just for fun. Even though we've seen it before, we still think he's got it wrong and killed Hades. Then, we're all laughing and pointing, because there's Hades' little nose and tiny eyes peeping up over Mystic Master Salvador's shoulder again, and the rat climbs up onto his head, us lot cheering 'till we piss ourselves.

That was his grand finale. Then it wasn't. Turns out all the stuff with cards and drawings and magic rats was just for starters, like he was just playing with us. He'd save the real magic to last.

If you dare to look straight at him, at his thin face, that Marie McGovern says is like Dracula, his eyes grow big as baseballs and he stares down, into your soul. Any mums still left after the rat murder trick, freak out and go off and browse the lacy knickers and bras dragging the little kids with them. Fine by us. Grown-ups have a lot of bad thoughts and none of them wanted Mystic Master Salvador knowing what was inside their heads, seeing into their souls, and knowing their dirty grown-up secrets.

He stares, with his laser eyes at, let's say, Brian Johnson. Brian's like 'oh oh, not me!' but loving it really, and just as Brian's head is literally about to explode and his brains fly all over the Star Wars stand, Mystic Master Salvador suddenly says, 'B'. We gasp and clap, there's no way Mystic Master Salvador knows Brian's name begins with B 'cos he doesn't know who Brian is. We worked out there was a 1 in 26 chance of getting it right, a bit less, 'cos Marie says no one has a name beginning with a Z or an X, at least no one in our town back then.

Mystic Master Salvador pretends to look up Brian in his big book of names. But we know Mystic Master Salvador is actually looking into Brian's soul. That's why the mums and dads hate Mystic Master Salvador. This is real magic.

Mystic Master Salvador reaches out his hand. The boys who get picked say you can't stop yourself, your legs walk for you, in your head, you're still standing with your mates in the crowd, but suddenly you're up on the stage, the cloak, the black curtains, you're part of the act. Brian's up on stage. Mystic Master Salvador puts a hand gently onto Brian's head, stroking his hair, getting ready. The boys that get picked say your brain gets hotter, you feel the thoughts streaming out your head, feel your soul emptying, like his long fingers are inside you, and that's how Mystic Master Salvador knows your name. He stares into the distance, all mesmerised, sucking the name out your head, suddenly he swings his burning eyes back onto you and clear and loud and for all to hear, he says, *'Brian!'*

We go mad. How does he do that? He doesn't know Brian and no way could he know his actual name!

I'd swap my Kevin Keegan Top Trumps card for that, to have that, to be up there. It did nearly happen once, his eyes swivelled across and stopped on me. Like he was noticing me for the first time. *'It's me!'* I stood strong and proud and ready for everything, his single eyebrow raised, and he picked Ashley Wilks instead. I still don't know what I did wrong.

I'd stare at him, pushing the first letter of my name at him, but I couldn't get picked, it was never me up on that stage. Instead, it would be Brian Johnson with the fastest serve in the year, Kevin Baker, the head boy, or Keith the teacher's son. Marie never got picked either, but she had black hair and was a girl so that explained it. I even tried not being interested at all, standing at the back, playing with the beaten up *try-before-you-buy* Etch-a-Sketch, shaking it again and again and again, and watching the black lines vanish, like they were never there. But that made me even more invisible.

Some kids never make it to the stage. Mystic Master Salvador sets eyes on them, and a dad yanks them off to look at the fishing rods and reels, and the silvery Day-Glo lures and sea hooks. Mystic Master Salvador watches those kids vanish from the toy section and disappear past the Clark's Shoes stand. We watch them go too, waiting for them to explode, or get struck by magic lightening, but that never happened. He spared them I suppose. He didn't seem to mind that the adults had all gone, and we liked that it was just us now.

It's weird that none of the grown-ups like Mystic Master Salvador. If they mention him, it's in a grown-up whisper. Maybe he *is* Dracula, and that's the big secret in town. I heard he did good things, was on the School Board, and other charity shit like that, did the books or kept the notes or something at the golf club or tennis club. I thought about how brilliant he'd be at the meetings, he'd already know what everyone was going to say, have the notes finished before the meeting started. You think they'd give him a medal, not go off and look at underwear and fishing rods on a Saturday.

I wanted to be his assistant, learn his powers. Then I'd know the answers to all the exam questions, top of the class with Kevin Baker. I'd get my own cloak, stand up there on stage, everyone waiting. Watching. I'd pick the new blond boy in town, the strange boy no one knew, summon him up on stage with my magic eyes, look into his head, see his thoughts. I'd name him, say his name out loud, and everyone would clap and cheer and we'd be up there, me and the new boy and he wouldn't feel so alone 'cos he'd been named.

The best bit, the bit that gives Mystic Master Salvador his credentials for being a major mind bender, is what happens at the very end. We're all clapping and laughing, he makes the boy take a bow, take all the applause, generous. Mystic Master Salvador does his bow, just with his head, and his eyebrow, he's not interested in anyone clapping his magic genius, and he gives a little smile, the only time he smiles. Makes him almost human.

Then. All of a sudden Mystic Master Salvador's cloak flies open, like he really is Dracula, the magic cloak engulfs the boy, wrapping him up, and the boy actually disappears! Gone! Then, just as quickly, Mystic Master Salvador disappears too, swishing through the black curtains at the back of the stage.

Even though this happened every week, through the whole summer, we always thought the boy had actually vanished, shot off into another galaxy, or vapourised. There'd be a sad family with an empty place at tea-time, beans on toast going cold.

A while later, the boy would reappear, looking like the blood had drained out his body. He'd reappear by the pick-and-mix counter, with a little paper-bag of melt-in the-mouth sherbet flying saucers or those see-through jelly babies to share. But none of us wanted one.

If the mums and dads knew what happened behind the curtain, then they weren't telling. That was the magic, no one really knew what they knew and what they didn't know.

The boys who disappeared had their minds melted, and their brains bleached clean. None of them could remember what happened. I'll never know, because Mystic Master Salvador, he never picked me. I'd name him, say his name out loud, and everyone would clap and cheer and we'd be up there, me and the new boy. I'd squeeze his shoulder and he wouldn't feel so alone 'cos he'd been named.

How Daddy Lost His Ear

Sallie Bingham

2nd Prize, Seán Ó Faoláin International Short Story Competition

---

"They were fighting," my cousin Tara tells me. She's the only person I've ever known named for a house. They went down to Georgia one time to find it but didn't. Torn down a long time before.

"They weren't fighting," I tell her. "Mama Blacksleeves took the truck and got stuck in the mud a yard from the house. Daddy was trying to help her get out."

"Those Blacksleeves always getting themselves into pickles," Tara says. We're sitting on the porch of our old house—this was years after it happened—and Tara being as nice as she is brought out some store-bought lemonade, too sweet for me but let that pass. Ever since my days at the Jesuit boarding school in Helena I've stayed off sweets and it wasn't something they told me, just instinct. I aim to stray strong.

At the time of this talk I was twenty-four, Tara a year younger. We're cousins, both breeds with white mamas gone since early. I take after Daddy, dark with the same long shiny hair I wear mostly braided. Tara's pretty like her mama, a Salt Lake City girl didn't care for the rez. I never expected Tara to stick around either but she found herself a boyfriend—Joe Pinchbelly, a Crow, we don't hold with that tribe but nothing was going to stop Tara once she fixed on him, visited him regular for two years at the prison down in Deer Lodge and married him soon as he got out. He's off working the oil patch now and so she come back home for company.

"So what happened?" Tara asks me, digging a loose cigarette out of her jeans pocket. She takes a while getting it to light with her pretty pink lighter.

I tell her, "Daddy got behind the truck to push and told Mama to rock it back and forth to get out of the mudhole. I was in the house, heard him shouting at her. She had the tires screaming, digging down deeper in the mud every time she stepped on the gas. Daddy was hollering at her to stop but I guess she didn't hear him 'cause she went right on trying to rock the truck. Flew backwards and knocked Daddy flat."

"Well, she didn't kill him," Tara says, not too fond of old Daddy, he always grabbing at her. "Caught him with the edge of the bumper and drove over his ear."

"How'd she do that?"

"The only part of him was under the tire."

She starts to laugh and I tell her to shut up. "You wouldn't of been laughing if you'd seen the blood. Bled like a stuck pig. I ran him on in the house, found some rags, bound up his head—"

"What about the ear?"

"Put it in a plastic bag and throwed it in the freezer. Got it out when I drove him down to the IHS and they sewed it on but crooked."

"How in the world!"

"I don't know but crooked it was and crooked it stayed, why he always wears his cap pulled low."

"Yeah but I saw that ear one time when he was coming out of the shower. Crooked as hell! Was he mad. Nothing for you to stare at, you little..." She runs down.

We both take a minute to look out over our field that's full of downed cornstalks left over from our last harvest five years before. After that with the drought we gave up on that field, all the good gone out of it once the spring dried up.

"What happened to Mama Blacksleeves?" Tara asks.

"She got out of the mudhole some way, drove on off, never did come back."

"Smart. Did your Daddy go after her?"

"No. Said good riddance. They didn't get on too well after the first month."

She nods. "He was still missing your mama."

"I doubt it."

"He always said she was prettier than anything else come down the pike."

"Pretty don't count much in the long run. She was always after him, do this, do that. A man can't hardly stand that kind of woman."

"Not if she's right," Tara says with the smirk that used to make me want to hit her. "Here he comes now." Daddy hit the cattleguard so hard coming through the gate we could hear it all the way to the porch.

I don't know what it is about Daddy but we both stand up when he comes up, toting a bag of booze. "You two go on in and clean up that kitchen," he tells us. "Godawful mess from last night." Hawk and them come over and we did party considerable.

We go in like he tells us, always have and always will, I guess. Tara fills a bucket and gets the mop—"Whew this thing stinks!"—and starts on the floor. I pick up dishes and stack them in the sink while Daddy unbags his booze and gets started with a few sips straight from the bottle. Tara fetches him a glass. He backhands it off the kitchen table and we watch it skitter across the linoleum. "When is that man of yours going to come back and make some babies for me?" he asks her.

"I'm not looking to make any babies for you, old man." She can be fresh.

Daddy reaches to grab her but she hops out of the way. "You with that crooked ear!"

He grabs his hat which he's taken off coming in and slaps it back on. "You want to stay in my house eat my food you watch your tongue, Bitch," he says.

"What food there is."

It's heating up. "I was telling how Mama Blacksleeve run over your ear," I says.

He starts laughing. He can do that any time. "She tried to tell me she was sorry!"

"I thought she hightailed it out of here."

"Did, but there's still the phone."

"Well, she did the right thing leaving," Tara says, pious as a church.

"You think I give a shit about that?" Now he is smooth, shiny, the way he can always get. "There's one thing a woman can do for me and one thing only and when she quits on that, I quit on her."

I've heard this story about a hundred times. "Why don't you go on in to the IHS, let them knock you out, take that ear off and sew it on straight?" I ask.

"I'm finished with that place. Last time I went they tried to stick that ass camera up me. Quit when I screamed. Like being fucked by a gorilla."

And there the three of us are laughing when there isn't a thing in the world to laugh about. But that's Daddy. There's people who hold things together and it's never the people you think it ought to be. Uncle Joe worked years at the sawmill, only drunk on Saturday nights, had a regular wife from Oklahoma, white and five half-white kids but he never could hold anything together while Daddy with his storming keeps the two of us in his house when we should have been long gone. Maybe waiting to see when his next shouting will happen, who will get slapped sideways, or maybe even waiting for the day he quits storming and starts acting like he cares, a day we both know is never going to come. But meantime he can always get us laughing.

Now he stops laughing first. "I'm peckish," he says with that lip curl we know means get something on the table fast. Tara goes in the kitchen, opens the freezer and digs out some buffalo burgers. Daddy always demands meat. She throws the patties in hot leftover pan grease in the skillet and Daddy and I go in the kitchen to watch the fat jump and spatter. I get out plates and forks—Tara makes me wash them, they was put away half dirty—and just when she's forking out those burgers we hear tires in the yard.

Daddy looks out the window and then I see his small smile. "Well look who's coming."

Tara keeps on putting out the meat but I go to the window and there's Daddy's red Ford truck parking by the stump. Mama Blacksleeves rolls out.

"You want her in here?" I ask Daddy but he's already throwing open the screen door and holding his arms out like they've been empty since she left three months before, which they have not.

Mama Blacksleeves runs up on the porch and then he has her grabbed up tight against his chest and they're both bawling. "Oh I missed you, Honey," Daddy says.

"How come you never called me?" she asks, black eye make-up shedding down her face with her tears.

Daddy never answers questions and so we don't know why he never called this woman he's grabbing so tight.

"Knew you'd come home when you was ready," he tells her, voice all gummed up with tears.

"Well I'm here now," she says, smearing her face on the back of her hand. "Tell your boy to get my stuff out of the truck."

I was already out the door and down the steps but then I had to holler back for the keys. Can you believe she'd locked Daddy's truck? She digs the keys out of her bag and throws them to me and then she and Daddy watch me unload a ton of her stuff, three green garbage bags full to bursting, two suitcases and some cardboard boxes.

"Where you want it?" I ask Daddy but she answers, smooth as silk, "Our bedroom, Sure Enough, thought you knew by now." They still call me that, claiming when I was little I said it all the time.

When I come back, Tara has the buffalo burgers served up with slices of paper towel for napkins and Daddy's special hot sauce and we all sit down and eat. I start to ask Mama Blacksleeves why she's come back but Tara gives me one of her looks. Daddy is talking about bringing in a bunch of cowboys to herd the mama cows up to the hill country for the summer and I want to say he won't need no cowboys because our old herd was sold off when the drought took the grass and the two we have left for old time's sake I can bring up without any trouble. I can do it myself but don't offer because Daddy says a man who offers before he's asked is a fool.

Tara drives off to her nurse class at the community college and Daddy and Mama go to their room and I shut my ears as best I can and start wrangling dirty dishes. When I've done as much as I aim to do I go out on the porch to smoke and look off toward the Kootenai where the trees are just leafing up. I might have closed my eyes for a minute and when I open them, here come Daddy and Mama grinning like a pair of cats.

"I guess you're back to stay a while," I say to Mama, a little bit more peeved than I have any right to be. She's not my mother, never has tried to boss me.

"Oh, for a while anyway," she says. "I'm aiming to go to L.A. in the fall."

Daddy give the hanging flesh on her upper arm a good pinch. "What's there we ain't got here, Darlin?"

"Everything," she says and she reaches up and traces that crooked ear with her finger. Daddy tries to swat off her hand but she won't let him and it seems to me I'm seeing something I've never seen before: Daddy smiling. Not grinning. Smiling the way you see an old dog smile when you give him a bone and I know Mama Blacksleeves is here to stay, at least till fall.

Late that afternoon when Tara comes back I tell her my thought but she don't believe me 'cause women never stay here except for her.

That evening Mama Blacksleeves and Daddy go down to Sheridan and won't be back till the bars close at 2am so Tara and I get settled comfortable, me in my sleeping bag on the floor and her on the bed. I never dispute that with her. Being a girl, she needs a bed with a sheet and a door with a lock while for me it's "immaterial"—that's a word I picked up somewhere and use pretty regular when things are heating up. I never have been one to fight about nothing and I like Tara and wish sometimes she weren't my cousin. I like her breasts, not big but shapely and she has no trouble showing them off in her thin shirts.

Daddy comes roaring and stamping in at some dark hour with Mama Blacksleeves trying to shush him. They step over me like I'm a log in the road and go in the kitchen and pull this and that out of the refrigerator. Daddy always comes back hungry from the bars.

He's cursing because all he can find is an old brown banana, some cheese and yogurt gone bad but Mama gets him to shut up and they trundle off to bed. After that things are pretty quiet till cockcrow when it all gets started again.

Daddy is going to drive down to the Burger King "before I starve to death" and the rest of us go with him, not that he's asked—he never asks—but we just know to go along, have gone along since we was big enough to walk. I mean the whole bunch of us, just Tara and me now but it used to be big brother Roberto (he's over in Iran) and Clinker who got shot dead in a bar fight a few years back and Norma who's married to a white man and gone. We were one big bunch then herded into the red truck to go somewhere, anywhere, with Daddy and he'd curse and say he never counted on no bunch of snotty-nosed kids but when we get to wherever he's going, he makes us get out and introduces us to everybody there. Bar, hardware store, feed store, fast food, it don't matter, he has friends everywhere and he wants them to know he has this bunch of kids. When we were little we'd be picking our noses or shuffling our bare feet in the dirt but one look from him and we'd straighten up and "fly right", hands at our sides and feet still and quiet. Now with just the two of us I wonder if he's going to do the same thing.

Well, it turns out he's going to the cemetery and I don't remember ever going there except when somebody was getting buried, like Clinker. He stops the truck by the fence and we climb out after him and follow him like little sheep through the gate. He heads to the far corner and Tara says, "He's been here before, he knows where he's going" and I have to say yes though I can't hardly imagine it. Next thing she'll have him coming with flowers.

Strides across to the far corner with us trailing after him and drops on his knees by this wooden cross. Tara pushes on my shoulder and I get down beside him and from there I can see the name and the dates in those block numbers I can't read.

Missy McKinley
Blessed Are The Pure In Heart

Mama Blacksleeves is getting down behind me, whispering to Tara, "Now who in the name?" but Daddy turns around and gives her a look and Tara knows better than to answer.

Anyway I don't expect she knows.

Daddy uses his sleeve to wipe some dirt off the cross. "Only white woman I ever loved," he says.

"I'm amazed to hear you say it," Mama Blacksleeves tells him and he leans back and gives her a swat. "None of your business, woman."

She's knocked back on her heels but rights herself and come out with, "Well, it was years before you and me met up."

Daddy is crossing himself and mumbling prayers, raised like all of us by the Jesuits. I doubt he remembers all the mumbo-jumbo but this he has down cold.

"Dust to dust ashes to ashes, Darlin," he says. "I'll be with you before you know it."

"Thought you were going to be buried up at the rez with Mamaw and Papaw," I say without thinking and then I get the back of his hand.

"You'll put me in the ground next to Missy!" he shouts and only Mama Blacksleeves is nuts enough to keep on arguing.

"You promised you'd go in the ground with me!" she shouts and he reaches back and rolls her.

Then we're all crying and pleading. "Shut up!" Daddy says and gets up off his knees and starts to the truck. "You're coming, come," he shouts over his shoulder and we're scrambling, knowing he'll leave us and it's a twelve mile walk home.

It doesn't end that way because Daddy is hungry again and so he drives to Burger King and treats us to Whoppers and milkshakes, whatever flavor we want, and by the time we get back in the truck, everything is peaceful.

*****

Till the next day. Mama Blacksleeves still feels like she's new (second time around) and that's when Daddy's women always go too far. After a few weeks they know they're old for him – second time around, third time around, it don't matter, they wear out on him fast.

Mama don't even have sense enough to wait till Daddy's had his coffee. She looks a mess, hair all tangled up from the night and every line in her face clear as graph paper in the morning light, no lipstick nor nothing but she starts right in.

"You know none of us is getting any younger," she says.

He grunts, wedging his right foot in his boot, getting ready to go.

"It's time we made plans," she says.

He wedges his left foot in his boot. "You always talk plans and you know I don't live my life that way." He stands up and stamps his feet down, his boots always too small and I know we're going to have a time getting them off end of the working day.

"Yeah but one of us could die anytime," Mama goes on and I know she's been practicing this speech, it comes out so calm and smooth but with a little hitch at the back of her throat tells me she's going to cry. I want to tell her, Don't cry, Daddy hates women's tears and I only remember one of them way back a skinny girl telling him when he said that, "Then don't make us cry." She was gone in twenty minutes.

He's heading out the door and Mama throws her last words over his head like a rope. "I'm going in town later sign my new will. I got some property," she says.

Daddy turns back at the door. "I don't want to hear about no 'property,'" he says. "I got twelve hundred and twenty acres here, more than I need or want."

"Yeah but I got mining rights on mine," she says, just about purring. Daddy never has been able to get ahold of the mining rights for this ranch, some rich cat from Denver bought them a long time ago before old Jake Bear knew what was going on.

She's caught his attention now and he hangs in the doorway watching her. "You planning on starting in the mining business?"

"Could be," she says. "My Daddy sold our rights on the mountain ranch to Colorado Old Mining and made a bunch of money."

"And tore up your ranch so nobody don't live there no more."

"What are you, one of them conservanists?"

He reaches to swat her but she ducks. "Never knew you to care about tearing up the land," she says, pleased as a kid with a candy bar.

"You'll come whining when they tear down your old house to get at what's under it," he says.

"It's going to be a lot of money, enough to build a big new house and then some."

She's riled him to where he's going to ask a question and that takes some doing. "You got plans for me too?"

She grins. "Maybe. Sit down and let's talk about it."

"I got to feed the horses," he says, out the door before she can stop him but I know it's not the end. She has that wild blind look in her eye like a horse heading to the barn and ain't nothing going to stop her.

"Let him eat before you start in," I tell her but she never has listened to me and don't begin now. So as soon as Daddy comes in the door at five, covered with the day's dirt and heading for the shower, she puts herself in his way and starts. "We get married I'll put you in my will," she says.

"I'll die first," he tells her and I hear from his tone he's been calculating.

" You let me start taking care of you you'll outlive us all."

"So what's my side of this bargain?" he asks her and I kind of admire the way she's pushed him this far.

"Just be nice to me," she says. She's been thinking this out for a while. "I don't count on you being faithful," she tells him with that hitch in the back of her throat.

"Not faithful but loyal," he says and I try to remember how many times I've heard him say that. I don't know why but with these women it never seems to get old.

"You'll want some girl and that's OK with me but you'll always come back," she says, making it not a wish but a promise.

"I'll think on it," he says and I'm amazed. He pulls off his shirt heading for the shower, and it's the first time I see his old man belly and the white hair on his chest.

I hear them disputing long into the night but they're in bed covered up to the eyes and I can't make out the words. Only he's not shouting and cursing and she's going on and on like a shallow stream bumping over rocks but still going.

I get to sleep before they do and in the morning I see her shaking out the blanket and smiling and I wonder what they agreed to if they agreed to anything and is this going to change my life.

Daddy is out early seeing to the well—it's running dry, looks like, and if it does we'll be finished here. I hear the pump groaning when it hits mud at the bottom and Daddy tells me to haul water from the cistern and pour it in the well and I do that all morning till the pump starts to work smooth. It's not a cure but it'll get us through the day with enough water for the horses and for the little bit of cooking Mama Blacksleeves might do and maybe there'll be rain soon and the well will fill. It's happened before but now we're into something different and the sun has that glare in it means no cloud is going to hinder it any time soon and it's way too hot for this early in the spring.

I don't know if it's the white hair on Daddy's chest or the big old man belly pushing on his belt but they do come out of it with something they can both put their names to—Daddy making his X—and Mama Blacksleeves is so pleased she goes around the kitchen putting something together for us and singing one of her old songs. Daddy shouts at her to stop the caterwauling and she laughs and lets it go cause now she has what she wants or nearly.

It turns out they got to have two witnesses to get it done legal at the Justice up in Fargo so Tara and I ride in the back seat of the pick-up for the long drive and nobody says a word the whole way like the whole thing would tumble down with just one word as a push. I know Daddy is in a foul mood cause he don't even light up and I never been on a long ride with him not smoking something and Mama Blacksleeves has the sense this time to say nothing. She's dolled herself up with the curling iron and enough make-up to paint a fence and somehow or another I start to feel sorry for her.

It's late afternoon by the time we get to the justice's office and he's just locking up and not pleased to have to open but Mama Blacksleeves don't give him any option and for once Daddy lets her take the lead.

The two of them stand up in front of the justice and he reads whatever from his book and I wonder why he's still got to read the words then remember nobody gets married around here so he's had no practice. Live together, yes, make some babies and then go off when it don't work.

The justice reads the words wrinkling up his nose like he smells something bad and I think he must of heard tales about Daddy but it don't matter now till he gets to the end and says, "Kiss the bride," and Daddy hollers, "What the hell!" and Mama Blacksleeves touches his arm and somehow lets him know it's OK to skip the kissing.

She shells out some bills to the Justice and he gets to the door and holds it open for us to go through and I say to Tara, "I never thought to see the day."

"He's a old man now," she tells me, "only reason it happened."

I want to think he maybe feels something about Mama Blacksleeves like now they'll be old together and can take care of each other when the time comes and won't have to go to the old people's home. I hold onto that for a while, six months maybe till Daddy comes home drunk and she says something to him about it and he smashes her jaw with his fist.

I drive her down to the IHS thinking she'll cry and blab the whole way but she never says nothing, never sheds a tear, and that's when I know whatever bargain she's made with Daddy is going to stick because he never could stand women's tears.

Then the first check comes from Colorado Old Mining and they go out to celebrate, dressed up and ready for the white people staring at them at the Ranch King where we never go ordinarily. It costs too much but with the check in Mama Blacksleeve's hand that ain't a problem and never is going to be.

They get back and Mama decrees they're going to live in her house other side of the rez and leave this wreck to Tara and me.

Tara says she's glad of a little peace and quiet but I miss the racket, the sex and the fighting, and it seems like the days have got longer and the nights too and I start getting ready to leave home and go somewhere, maybe Denver where I hear they're building night and day and I can get a job in construction.

I go back for their Silver or whatever—Mama Blackleeves says they don't have time to count it off in the years so she turns the years into months and that way it looks like they'll get to Gold and she'll have Daddy in a suit for a big celebration.

Tara always says it's Daddy getting old that did it but I think it's when his ear got tore off and sewed back on crooked.

The Price of Cattle

Mattie Brennan

I was nine years old and sitting in the passenger seat of my father's red Landcruiser. We were on our way to sell a pair of heifers at the mart in Ballina, towing a trailer my father had borrowed from our nearest neighbour at the time, Tom Mullarkey. As we lurched by the shore of Lough Talt, the trailer clanged and the heifers lowed. The Landcruiser's engine grumbled as we climbed through the Windy Gap. When we reached the crest of the hill, a clutch of horned sheep crossed our path and walked down an embankment on the other side of the road. Their fleeces were scraggly, and they each had red spots on their rear ends. I asked my father why wild sheep would need such markings.

They're not wild, he said. They're mountain sheep. Why don't we have sheep, daddy? I said. He laughed and said, We're poor enough with only the cows, Desmond. The last thing we need is a flock of them yokes.

On the outskirts of Ballina town, children were playing in a schoolyard. My mother had let me skip school that day but only because the Christmas holidays were around the corner. As she fixed my coat that morning she had whispered to me, You won't be making a habit of this. Now, look after that fella and let ye come straight home after the mart, all right? And remember, Desmond, those heifers are for your benefit more than ours.

In the mart my father put me standing at the edge of the parade ring and told me to stay till he returned. I asked how long he'd be but he didn't reply. I stood on my own with my head barely above the parapet, watching heifers, weanlings and bulls being led around by a man wearing a white coat like a scientist's only his was streaked with muck. A brown Simmental bull with dark, fierce eyes lifted its tail and let a line of shit fall to the ground. I held my nose but still the stench was rancid.

My father eventually returned. A man standing near us with a narrow, lined face nodded at him. Many beyond? the man said. A fair crowd, said my father. I might go over for a hot one to warm the bones before I head home, said the man. Have you far to go? The other side of Belmullet. You'd need more than one before setting off for there.

The man laughed, and my father looked down at me and smiled. He blew into his cupped hands and said, She's chilly, but our trip won't be for nothing. The prices are good today. And look what I found. He handed me half a packet of Silvermints. When he breathed close to me I smelled traces of whiskey as well as mint.

Mammy will be happy the prices are good, I said, and put a sweet into my mouth. My father's smile faded. What did she say? he said. She said we're to go straight home, and she said that the heifers are more mine than yours. He laughed, ruffled my hair and spat into the parade ring. Someday they will be, he said.

We stood in silence till our heifers were paraded. The man in the white coat jerked on two ropes and circled the perimeter of the ring, dragging the stumbling heifers behind him. My father made his way over to another man who reached in and slapped the heifers' haunches.

Soon afterwards we sat in the Landcruiser, waiting for the frosted windows to clear. My father counted out fourteen blue notes that all said £20 and had a picture of Yeats on them.

Teacher said he's the most famous Sligoman ever and we should all be proud to come from the same place as him, I said. You don't come from the same place as him, my father said. He was from the north of the county where the land is topping and where farmers don't have to scrimp and save. It might as well be a different planet, Desmond. Sure we'd all be poets if we'd the luxury of good land.

We drove out of Ballina. I was getting hungry. I asked my father what he thought mammy would make for dinner but he didn't answer. He was looking far ahead, and I thought he might be sad that the heifers he'd raised since they were calves were no longer his.

In the village of Bonniconlon, he slowed down and parked.

We'll have a little celebration, he said. We'd a grand day.

I shook my head no but he said, One won't do any harm. Now come on and have a drink with your auld man.

The pub was small. There was a fire whose flames threw licks of light across a dusty cement floor. The place smelled like our kitchen when my grandfather was alive and used to sit in the corner smoking his pipe.

Three old men sat at the bar. They turned around and nodded. A barman with big grey eyebrows like Brillo pads said, Dessie, how're things?

Mighty, sure, said my father. I'll have a pint of stout and a half-one, and the young buck will have a Cidona and a bag of Tayto.

The barman brought me the bag of crisps and a big bottle of Cidona and left them on the bar. My father lifted me up, so I was sitting beside the three old men. He went to the toilet.

The old man closest to me wore the same type of flat cap that Tom Mullarkey always wore. He swallowed the dregs of a pint, looked towards the toilet door and said to the barman, Not this fucken dose again.

I felt the barman's eyes glance at me, but I pretended to read the back of the crisp packet. Arrah, he's grand, Jim, the barman said to the old man. 'Course you'd say that, said the old man. Doesn't he leave you a few bob? He nearly burst my head the last time going on about the win in Malta. Kept saying can you believe we're off to Italy. As if I care about that auld foreign sport? Ground football, it's only a load of bollocks.

The barman's eyes narrowed and he tilted his head towards me. The old man grunted then turned to me and said, That's a big drink for a small man. What class are you in? Third class, I said. Who's your teacher? Ms Sheedy. What's she like? She's lovely. But has she a lovely chassis?

His howls of laughter turned into a coughing fit, his face like a red balloon about to burst. You deserved that, Jim, said the barman, smiling. You're an awful terror.

My father came back and sat down. He drank all the whiskey in one swoop and sucked in a breath through closed teeth. I asked him what a chassis was. The three old men erupted into laughter. The barman's eyes flitted left and right. My father straightened and said, What's that about? The men quietened. Nothing at all, Dessie, said the barman. Jim here was just trying to educate the boy. He's the smartest child in his school, my father said. No need for ye bucks to teach him anything. He winked at me then and whispered, It's the underside of the Landcruiser. I'll show you sometime.

This is your young fella? the barman said. He is, said my father. The barman smiled at me and said, And will you be a farmer one day like your daddy? Begod he will, said my father. He has to. He's the only child God graced us with.

He swallowed the rest of his pint and left it on the counter. Cream slid down the inside of the glass. I jumped off the chair, but he put his hand on my shoulder and said, Don't be rushing. But mammy said to go straight home, I said. And the dinner might be ready. I'm sure there's a good fire going with the turf I saved, he said. The dinners won't go cold.

He drank three more pints after that. I tried to save my crisps for later that night, but after a while I ate them and then tore the bag apart and licked the salty crumbs. When my father finished his fourth pint he left a note on the bar and the barman gave him some change. The old men threw up one hand each when we were leaving, but they didn't look around.

It was dark when we sat into the Landcruiser. While we waited again for the windows to clear, my father crouched forward and tucked his hands into his armpits. I opened my mouth and watched my clouds of breath hang in the air. He looked over and said, Isn't it great to be young and not feel the cold? I wasn't cold, but my stomach was frantic with hunger.

We drove slowly out of the village, the road sparkling before us. The Windy Gap was foggy. My father leaned forward, squinting and gripping the steering wheel tight. The radio crackled as we lost reception. He turned the volume down to nothing. The empty trailer rattled a little, but everything seemed quiet, as though the fog had muffled all sound.

Suddenly, I saw a flash of red and white in front of us, then a set of eyes like shiny beads. My father wrenched the steering wheel to avoid hitting the sheep. We slid towards the opposite edge of the road and he braked and we were thrown forward and a loud crash boomed and the Landcruiser stopped dead.

Blood gushed from my father's nose. My hands hurt from where I'd held them against the dashboard, but I wasn't bleeding like him. We got out. The trailer was at an odd angle and its back hung over the verge of the road. The back window of the Landcruiser was smashed.

Fucken jackknifed, said my father. I'll have to take it off and put it back on properly. He wiped some blood from his nose and blew into his hands and then unhitched the trailer. He tried to pull it towards the hitch but it slipped away from him and he couldn't grab it in time and it rolled off the road and went tumbling down the embankment.

He held his head in his hands and roared, Fuck it. Fuck it, anyway.

We drove the rest of the way home in silence, the only noise coming from the wind as it swept through the shattered back window.

When we pulled into the backyard my father said, Go on in, Desmond. Not a word to your mother yet. I'll follow you in soon.

My mother was in the kitchen, sitting near the range and reading a book. Slowly, she placed a bookmark between two pages, got up and left the book on the table. I thought ye were coming straight home? she said. We almost hit a sheep but daddy swerved just in time, I said. I felt my face getting hot as my mother stared at me but didn't speak. My father walked in.

I'm perished, he said. Is the grub warm? My mother placed her hands on the edge of the table, as if she needed to support herself or she might collapse. It's cremated by now, she said. Where did you stop? I hope you didn't have more than two pints and your son along with you?

Only the two, he said. He went to the range and took out two plates with mashed potatoes and lamb chops and peas and gravy.

A crust coated the gravy and mashed potatoes and the meat was tougher than leather, but still I ate like a *banbh.* My mother sat back in the armchair. I couldn't see her face because she held the book in front of it. After some time, she said, Well, how'd they go? Middling, said my father. Can't complain.

A kettle, resting on top of the range, started to whistle. My mother carried it over to the worktop behind where we sat. I heard the clinking of mugs and then a gasp. I turned around and saw her looking out at the broken window of the Landcruiser. Light from a bulb above the back door made the speckles of broken glass glisten.

What happened to the Landcruiser? she said. Accidents happen, said my father. The fog was wicked and, anyhow, the Landcruiser is the least of our worries. What do you mean? she said. I mean we'd an awful close one and we lost the trailer down the Windy Gap. What? You heard me, woman. Oh Lord save us, Tom'll be livid. It'll be fine, I'll get him another one. That'll cost a fortune, Dessie.

My father's hands tightened as though he was trying to bend his knife and fork. We'll manage, he said. My mother shook her head and said, You just had to stop in for porter, didn't you? Even when your son is famished with the hunger you couldn't come straight home. Well you can forget about him missing school ever again. My father pushed his chair back, stood upright and faced her. All the toil I put in, he said, can I not stop for a couple of pints on mart day? And Desmond had to learn the way of things. What would you have us do with the place otherwise? Let it turn to ruin? It wouldn't be missed if it did, she said. You're nothing but a miserable cunt, he said.

My mother inhaled a short, sharp breath. There was a silence, and my eyes started to burn with tears. I made to run for my room but, at the doorway, I stopped and turned and pointed at my father.

Daddy lied, I shouted. He had whiskey as well as four pints, and the prices for the cattle were better than middling.

My father looked at me. His nose was slightly swollen and his mouth was wide open. He looked as if I'd winded him with a vicious punch.

A few long moments passed when I wondered if I'd ruined everything, so when Tom Mullarkey rapped at the back door and shouted hello, I was delighted at the distraction. My mother told my father to stay where he was and she went out to Tom. I sat at the kitchen table again. My father went to the range, opened the door and stoked the turf with a poker. Flames rose like flaying orange ribbons.

Outside, Tom Mullarkey was talking to my mother but I couldn't hear what they said. My father closed the range door, held one palm over his eyes and made a sound like one of our heifers sometimes made. It was like a grunt, low and sore, that seemed to come all the way up from his gut.

Tom burst in the door and my mother came following after him, grabbing his elbow, saying, We'll get you another one, Tom. It was an accident. He shrugged her off and said, God love you, but I don't know how you stick it. He turned to my father then and said, You better get me a new trailer and there'll be no borrowing of it, do you hear me, Dessie? The fog was wicked, Tom, said my father. If you hadn't drink taken you'd be able for the fog. I took no drink. Come off it, do you think I came down in the last shower?

Tom jabbed a long, bony finger towards my father and stepped closer to him. Calm down, Tom, said my father. You should've seen the fog. The fog! said Tom. The fog! You have an excuse for everything, Dessie. You're clean fucken useless is all you are.

Tom shook his head and turned to storm away but as he neared the door my father took a few brisk steps towards him and drew the poker back and swept it through the air in a wide arc and caught Tom flush on the side of the head. Tom fell in a neat clump onto our kitchen floor. His hat fell off and landed by my mother's feet. There was a mark on his temple like a berry stain. He was killed instantly.

******

There is a thick layer of mildew on the windscreen of my father's old Landcruiser. As I walk towards it the wintry sunshine bathes it in a brilliant light. It's been laid up behind my parents' dilapidated shed for years, its once-red paint now a faded pink.

Moss grows out of its grill and its four flat tyres sit on tufts of grass. Flakes of rust hang from the rims of the windows. I reach out my hand and break away a piece. It crumbles like a dead leaf, turning my thumb and forefinger a vivid orange. I close my eyes, bring my finger to my nose and inhale the ferrous smell.

I go into the house. My mother is sitting in the armchair reading the novel I gave to her the last time I was here. The radio is on high volume, drowning out my father's rheumatic groans from down the hallway. He lies in bed every afternoon for an hour, a routine he never got out of after his release. I have a cup of tea with my mother and tell her I better get going back to Dublin. She asks me if I'll stay the night but I tell her I've a pile of papers to correct at home.

And when I put my head around the door of my father's room to say goodbye, he remains lying on his side with his back to me. Safe driving, Desmond, he says over his shoulder. Fair play for visiting. It does always make your mother's day.

My First Job
Helen Flynn

Exasperated, I snarl at my eldest, "Would you ever do me the courtesy of bringing down your laundry so as I can fuck it into the drum of the goddamn washing machine, please and thank you".

Eleven years old…

Before your age Oisín, I was out there working, quite literally for my bread and board. I learned to split from my body, leaving it in order to tolerate my young life's traumas. Alrighty, admittedly a tad heavy a disclosure in the midst of a Friday evening bollicking from mum. My eye rolling, woke child, a most unsympathetic witness to my bloodletting.

But boy does laziness offend me. I never knew laziness as a child. Innately we understood it to be a mortal sin, one that our souls would suffer hideously for in the long wait at purgatory. Best to be avoided at all costs! Today that same inertia prods and antagonises a sleeping and grotesque rage from deep within me. Flashes of rage that come from a seed planted in a time of great darkness so cold nothing else could possibly grow. A fire once awoken boils and courses through my veins causing me to clench my jaw, tongue deliberately held hard to the roof of my mouth, a concentrated yank up of my pelvic floor, toes squirming, fists scrunching, knot my legs, cross my bony fingers in the vain hope of restraining, constricting the damn wildness of the surge of emotion from painful memories.

I was seven years young when left into the Airne Villa orphanage ran by the Mercy order of nuns carrying on the good and dutiful work of their founder Sr. Catherine MacAwley. The orphanage dominated the Rock Road. The Rock being the Lady of Lourdes grotto that rose boldly as gatekeeper to the heavenly beautiful town of Killarney, casting her long shadow over the ecclesiastical epicentre of all of the kingdom of County Kerry. I remember that first night, forty years ago as if no time has since passed. It was pitch black without a moon or as much as a star in the night sky to offer solace on the long and eerie taxi journey to the orphanage. The pungency of overzealously heated milk hung in the air, rivalling the dirty hanging skins on the rim of the bath I'm now ushered into. The standing water already performed its evening role as sheep dip to the sleeping children already in their beds. I step into the water, fully clothed, I never meant to be a bother or cause such an explosive outrage of anger and disgust. We were from the sticks, plucked down from the side of a Kerry mountain. We'd never had running water, we shat and pissed outside like Taoists. We didn't have as much as a change of clothes either, in fact I was in my nightdress earlier that same week at school, which was one of the many reasons I now found myself here, wherever in the name of god, here was?

From that night forth, at bath time, a rotation of older boys would take their turns to hide behind the bathroom door to pounce and gag me from behind. Their strength effortlessly clasping my wrists together as if to arrest me, then shoving my ridget and fidget vessel up against the sink so as he could savour his naked captive in the mirror while my head hung in the deepest mortification and repulsion. It's futile to struggle, I just suffer it out until he finishes his enthusiastic wank.

The order was revered for establishing a number of community enterprises. One such was the Mercy Laundry where I now served for my first summer after fourth class in primary school. All week long from Monday to Friday with a half day on Saturday to allow for confessions and Sunday, why Sunday was why the world existed at all. A childhood never graced the time to wander, wonder and dream, every moment scheduled for labour and servitude.

It was the summer of '86, and Madonna's 'True Blue' album rang out from the radio. Arm in arm, skipping down the nuns' Rosary Lane linking the orphanage to the convent grounds, merrily we sang out, 'Like a virgin, touched for the very first time.' We sensed it was a little naughty but we're in no way curious as to know how or why? Maura Higgins of 'Love Island', with her 'Fanny Flutters' would have gone well over our divinely innocent heads in those days. It was many many years later, before it dawned on me at all, why on earth Sister would visit me at night. Her ominous shadowy outline with her veil off would frighten the bejayus right out of me, as she gently disturbed my sleep to raise both my arms from my sides onto my chest in a 'criss cross, Playtex know your heart' kind of way. With eyes now open from the wet of holy water I'd watch her silently glide across the bedroom to repeat the action on the other children. She needn't have worried, none of us girls ever managed to masturbate, it was taken from each one of us long before we ever knew of it.

The flat roofed utilitarian laundry sat on the grounds of the impressive convent and nunnery, an eight-bay windowed, two storey gothic revival style splendour, built on a quadrangular plan about a courtyard with a dormer attic with a peep hole window perched high from where Sr. Pius, most fuckin pious indeed, patrolled and performed the morning's head count and roll call from her eagle's vantage.

Beginning our day with 7am mass in the convents chapel, amongst the 'no faced' shrinking standing stones and dying mothy nuns, we knelt in solemn prayer. I was a spritely child, and eager to showcase my mastery over long and complicated prayers with a sometimes Brian Blessed enthusiasm. I was happy to trade my devotion for the glow of attention.

Then a brisk return to the orphanage for breakfast, overseen by our forever pacing and praying mother superior Sr. Alphonus, she had the everlasting duty of praying for the sins of our mothers. Although I never did learn what those sins were.

My dutiful mother lost her virginity on her wedding night with a knife held firmly to her throat, and when the full extent of his psychotic alcoholic brutality became impossible to survive, she knelt at the feet of her father and two brothers in the gutter of the family farm pleading for refuge in the days long before the mercy of divorce, but instead of Christian compassion and charity she was beaten so badly that she was never to recover. It would have been kinder to have allowed her to die that night, but instead she was cruelly condemned straight to hell. Never ever again would she be allowed to hold her precious eleven-month young baby girl, still suckling from her chest. Birthed, poignantly on her very own birthday and lovingly christened her very own name, Teresa. She never again got to look into the eyes of her adored blue eyed, blonde little three-year-old cherub, her only son, nor did she ever again get to hold the hand of her first born, me. She didn't even get to say goodbye and spent her remaining decades as a ghost in psychosis roaming the streets of the towns and villages, woods and mountains of Kerry calling out for her taken children. That's when she wasn't in a straitjacket in the padded cells of the notorious and terrifyingly inhumane St. Finan's psychiatric lunatic asylum, which hauntingly loomed only a stone's throw from the orphanage where we were now separated for life.

Sr. Alphonus supervised like Roald Dahl's tyrannical 'Miss Trunchbull' but unlike Matilda none of us kids possessed the telekinesis required to escape the utter lack of autonomy we now had over our lives. Slopping us up a porridge they'd cry out for in the plastering trade, we again returned for work, hard men's work.

An assembly of baskets as large and deep as the ocean, rolled out heaped with miles of tangled wrung starched sheets, icebergs mounted like meringue peaks. Then came the synchronised Morris type dance of four young maidens as we shook out the finest thread-count of sheets from each corner. It was our Olympic sport, and god protect us the youngest and littlest of sacrificial lambs being paired up with the older impatient local women. Women with faces grey and creviced from years of steam, starch, fags and very little else.

It was often their only opportunity to make physical their pent up frustrations, and so with glee, they'd give a violent shake with the sole intention of reefing out the corner of the sheet from my hand. This would cause a flurry of rescue like the Eucharist being accidentally dropped and a gaggle of altar boys rushing to attend the scene. We couldn't risk impurities onto our most beautiful of sheets, sheets destined for the arse of our neighbour the bishop Diarmaid Ó'Súilleabháin and all the arses of his clergy. Yes, the filthiest of sinful sheets in all of Killarney town made virginal once more.

As the runt of the litter the initiation I dreaded most was a wicked whip of the corner of the sheet masterly aimed at the eyeball before you had time to blink, causing you to drop like a man kicked brutally square in the balls. But you had to fall in silence, suppressing the natural urge to whelp and cry out. You never ever call out… NEVER.

Paused, we'd stand at our workstations in silence for the twelve noon Angelus, I'd close my eyes, futilely fight back and lick my salty tears, bask in my daily private audience with the mother of all mothers, 'Forgive them for they do not know what they are doing,' she naively reassures me.

Then dinner, a hurried silent routine, and a return to work. We'd stand at either side of the gigantic steaming roller, a product of the industrial revolution. Perched on footstools and working in pairs, the trick was to hold on tight to your corner of the sheet and pull it taunt like stretching a canvas. We carefully lined up the corner to be fed into the press, much hotter than the one hundred degrees Celsius required for water to boil. Then came the blast of angry steam, scalding my nostrils.

Basins of iced water to cool the malicious skin burns, but the lower skin layer continued to burn right throughout the night, with only my well-worn bottom lip to offer suck. The sheets miraculously emerged dry and stiffened, a sacred sight to behold, a privilege and again the beautiful waltz of folding to godliness perfection. The tips of my fingers now hardened with angular calluses not belonging on a child's hands but I'm able to rat-a-tat-tat a tune on any wooden surface.

Supper, six o'clock another genuflection for the Angelus. Then the marathon, the rosary, a feverish exaltation of devotion. I fuckin' loved it. Here I shone with my proud proclamations: like giving great head, I gave a great Apostles Creed. The rise and fall and pace of praying led to climax after climax. Bernini's sculpture, 'The Ecstasy of Saint Therase' made real.

Night after night, we knelt in tidy rows, facing an altar to the Holy Family. We were like penned in sheep, the parameters patrolled by wolves with praying hands that quickly turned rosary beads into knuckle dusters in response to any sideways glances. Often I'd have to kneel beside some fucker I'd later in the evening have to fight off me in the dark. If only I'd had the cop on of Lorena Bobbitt in those days eh. It wasn't meant to be, but a 'freeze or fawn' kinda kid I was.

Fixating on a spot in the rooms dominating Byzantine painting, I concentrate my gaze. Holding the crucifix of our beads, the first of three mysteries were announced, each hosting five glorious decades of rosary. The littlest in their hand-me-down onesies were always the first to fall. They were too young for a Nativity play, and their bellies too empty for this endurance test of both will and form. The trancing and hypnotic sway of kneeling children, devoid of rebellion, submissive renunciates of all worldly possessions calling out religious responses far in advance to our understanding of language was without doubt a most unnatural state.

It was here in this glasshouse, this microcosm of self-serving survival, brother separated from sister, and sister pitted against sister, and children torn from their mothers, aunties, grannies and cousins and expected to forget that they had ever come from them at all, it was here that I was first groomed to believe I was the lowest piece of worthless scum in all of God's forsaken family.

Poor auld Oisín looks up at me from the washing machine. "Ah Mum, it's Friday, would you chill out?"

"History is rarely told by the Antelope," I bark.

"It's a good job you're a fuckin' Lion then, mum," he quickly counters.

You know, normally, I'd tell him right off for the swearing, but I think we can agree for today, he's made a fair point.

Gretchen
Emma O'Donoghue

Gretchen sat in the back of the car waiting for her father. He had driven them over to a builders' yard in Lucan to pick up some four-by-twos and a few other things. The yard belonged to his friend Paddy Mulligan, who sometimes came to their house. Lucan was on the other side of the city from where they lived, and the surroundings were unfamiliar: a lot of big trees, high stone walls and houses that looked different to theirs.

On her lap was a copy of Grimm's Fairy Tales, a dog-eared paperback, its cover entirely missing. She searched through it for one of her favourites, about a maid who was waiting for her master to return with a guest for dinner. The maid was roasting two chickens on a spit and kept tasting them and running down to the cellar to take draughts of beer. So vivid were the details that Gretchen could both smell and taste the roast chicken (her mother always cooked a chicken on Sundays) and imagine how refreshing the beer must be, though she was too young for beer and sensed that she wouldn't like the hoppy taste; she knew what beer looked and smelled like because her father brewed it at home in the kitchen, in a yellow plastic bin. Her father sometimes drank Guinness and allowed her to taste the creamy head, which disappointingly did not taste like cream but more like the top of a wave in the sea, and sometimes he came into her room in the morning carrying a glass of something foaming which he said was "Andrews", which also did not taste as good as it looked.

Her favourite part of roast chicken was the skin; it was hard to resist pulling it off straight away when it came out of the oven. Last Sunday when she'd been fidgety in Mass, her mother had told her that she'd get no chicken for lunch (she didn't want any hairy old chicken anyway, she'd answered back, although she did). Her mother was short-tempered and tired all the time now because she was having another baby soon; her stomach was huge and she spent most of the day in her dressing gown, which wasn't normal. Gretchen half-hoped the new baby would be a girl because she already had three brothers. But her father sometimes told her she was special because she was the only girl, so she wasn't sure how she felt about it.

She found a sweet in her cardigan pocket and unwrapped it. It must have been there since she'd had mumps a couple of months ago. In the morning she had been afraid to say that she felt awful because her mother was so irritable, and she'd tried to swallow her cornflakes. Then her mother had noticed her swollen cheeks and felt her forehead, and her voice and face had changed, and she'd said, "Go back up to bed, I'll get the doctor." It turned out that the cure for mumps was sucking hard sweets! She'd had a couple of weeks off school and had spent most of the time in bed reading library books.

Her father had been unwell for a couple of days recently too. He had fainted at work, and he'd had to go to the hospital to have some tests; she'd heard her mother talking about it on the phone afterwards. He was better now. He put on his blue tracksuit every morning and went out running, while her mother moved around the kitchen in her dressing gown with the flowers on it, going between cooker, sink and table, while the sunlight bounced off the yellow flowers on the wallpaper, while her brothers thumped about in their room upstairs, while the autumn leaves dropped from the trees in the garden.

Gretchen looked out through the back window of the car. She could see the builders' yard at the end of the road, its gate standing open, but there was nobody around. She considered playing with the cigarette lighter in the dashboard, which she had been told not to touch, and decided against it. Instead she opened her book and started reading "The Goose-Girl." Falada, Falada: the name and its repetition gave her a strange feeling. When she'd finished the story, she noticed that it was now beginning to get dark. She turned her head to look through the back window again and saw Paddy Mulligan walking slowly towards her with a policeman.

Papio

Marius Padurean

Everything I have to say is about this kid, Papio, who lived in our building, at the ground floor and had a crap family, and who one day disappeared, and was never heard of again. His father was a violent drunk. The mother went through all these nut houses in the country, and none could cure her of her insanity. His sister had this loser of a boyfriend who couldn't rub two nickels together and stole crap from people to sell for nothing. Papio didn't really care about all this. His father scared him shitless, but beyond that, he cared about nothing. At times not even about the beatings. The father would come home from work dead drunk and would run after Papio through the apartment all night to beat his ass. He loved punching his son in the face. Papio had white, almost pinkish skin, like marble, with light brown freckles, around his nose and eyes and by the time his father was done with him, his face was rainbow colored. He never bruised like all of us when our parents beat us up. His skin would become colorful. He told me that while his father would punch his face, he would at the same time be screaming at his wife, who wasn't there, and he probably imagined it was her that he was punching. No one really understood why Papio put up with this crap every day. But I knew.

The first time I spoke to Papio was in the summer of '89.
He offered to give me a bike ride to the river. I didn't have a bike back then and was constrained to be with all the losers down in the street, kicking ball. Boys in our neighborhood who had bikes, rode out of the city to the river for a swim, as the heat, especially in July, would go up to 45°C.
So, anyway, that summer I was playing ball, as I said with the nobodies, behind our building, when Papio comes up to me and says:
Wanna ride with us to the river?
I didn't swim (I'll tell you that story later), but I really wanted to be with them, so I said yes.
You need to tell your grandma or something?
I wasn't allowed to leave the neighborhood, especially without asking permission. But I said I needn't tell her anything.
And so we went.
From where we lived to the river was about 12-15 kilometers. When we got there my ass was numb as I had to sit on Papio's rack platform, at the back of the bike.

Quite a pain in the ass not to have a bike of your own? Papio joked.
At that time, I thought it was funny.
In the gang there was this guy whom Papio christened 'Buttcheek'. He had a round face, and his right cheek was considerably larger than his left.
Based on his own joke, Papio asked Buttcheek what he thought of the whole deal.
What do you think, he said.
It's shit.
Everyone fell on their faces laughing.
That's how things were back then.

Papio was full of ideas. Thinking about it now, in those days I believed that it was only God and Papio that truly knew the world around us, and by that, I mean the city. For example, the river flowed under two very old, suspended bridges, a car bridge and a train bridge. Papio's diving place was from the middle of the car bridge. We would leave our bikes at the head of the bridge and walk on the side to the middle. There, we would climb the rail and pass to the other side. Now you were twenty meters above the water, with nothing between you and it, just air. For a kid this makes an impression, believe me. Papio jumped first and would indicate to the rest where not to jump. He knew everything about the river, the way he knew everything about the cinema, but more about that later. One time he told us about this kid, who jumped headfirst directly into one of the old pylons, from a previous bridge, hidden in the water. His head exploded on impact. For a couple of minutes, the shadow of the bridge on the water became red. Then it was gone. Like everything else.
That was Papio. All ideas came from him or were run by him – what we did as a group, where we went, whom we took with us, that kind of stuff. He had many ideas and had many stories to tell. Papio would tell stories all the time. Come to think about it now, everything had to be a story we could share with others at the end. We were his apostles. He fed on movies, that was his source of life. When he was not roaming the neighborhood, the forest or some other place around town in search of adventure with the gang, he was at the cinema. Sometimes seeing the same movie a dozen times.
I told you before I knew why Papio refused to leave his dad, and just be on his own somewhere. The cinema in our neighborhood kept him there.

None of us knew Papio's age. We knew he was older than the rest of us, but that was it. Anyway. In his presence you felt safe. There are no more kids like Papio, today.
One day he freaked us all out. We were all playing in the street when we heard these screams. Buttcheek came running and screaming that this guy from the towers beat him up, just behind the cinema.

Papio said nothing. He just got up and started walking towards the cinema. We followed him. Chelu, the guy who beat Buttcheek was there seating on a bench in front of his building. Papio took a rock and split Chelu's face in two. He looked like shit. He fell to the ground holding his face, screaming. The skin on his face exploded, and blood was everywhere.
If you touch 'Buttcheek' again I will kill you.
That's all he said.
Anyway, what is clear is that without Papio, our childhood would not have been the same. Maybe not even our lives after that. But all this is not something we could have known back then.

In those years everything was dirty. Apartments, buildings, neighborhoods, the city, the people, especially children. Everything, including people, had holes, worn edges, moldy walls, broken windows, floors that looked like unfinished puzzles. Even the sky was dirty. On some days the sky reflected the city, with its gray narrow, dirty streets, dark, and leading nowhere. As a kid you see stuff like this, believe me.
And inside this universe, on Gladiolus, the main street in our neighborhood, among the ten storied towers, slept a concrete giant, on his knees, in whose concrete belly, in the dark, on a dirty white rubber-like placenta, spread out on a wall, stories were being born, and people went in and sat on chairs in the dark, and watched them.
This was Papio's world and obsession. His favorite movie was Speed, with Sandra Bullock and Keanu Reeves.
You know, some kids are into amusement parks or video games, of which we had neither, or some love a quiet evening with their parents or a campfire on the mountain. Led by Papio, we worked our way into the dark, like miners, into the megalith's belly, through tunnels and corridors, looking for stories.
Now it must be said, not all in the group were into this. The risk of being caught was high. Most were afraid. So much so, that in the end, only Papio and I remained. None really understood what Papio was about and his passion for movies.
Some of the boys were afraid of the dark, some of being caught. But as I myself discovered at the end, after Papio vanished, fear was fear, no matter what generated it.
The cinema was owned by two twin brothers, midgets, with similar names, which I can't remember now. Either one or the other sat in the booth outside every day and sold tickets. In all those years, until Papio's disappearance, I never paid to see a movie. Papio had secret entrances and methods to enter the much-desired belly of the beast.

Papio's mother was a crane operator at this forge outside of town, the same forge where his father worked. Many parents from the neighborhood worked there and all children believed it to be a cursed place. Between us, back then, all jobs were cursed. All parents came out doomed from that sliver of history... The curse of the factory that drove both men and women to the bottle, the curse that kept both fathers and mothers poor and wretched, was the curse that made many orphans. Being cursed back then was catching, like smallpox. We all came out of those years with scars.

There were all kinds of stories in the neighborhood about Papio's mother. One was that up in her cabin, on the crane, she could see far, so far that she actually saw the life she was supposed to live. And since that day her desire and passion for that life grew so much that she could do nothing else but visualize that life in her mind. She was trapped. It was the moment when she lost her mind. She travelled there, the trip lasted only a second and it stayed. She remained there in that cabin for a long time. When the next shift came the day after, they didn't know how to bring her down. Her eyes were fixed on the horizon. Nobody really knows how they brought her down. There were tears in her eyes and since that day she didn't speak again. I only bring this up about his mother because it reminds me of Papio when he watched a movie at the cinema. He was transfixed, transported into another world. At the sanatorium she would go through long stretches of time, days, weeks, without moving an inch. She would see through walls, ceilings, roofs. Her gaze fixed on the point at the horizon where children were laughing, and families were happy.

I said earlier that I was going to tell you the story of why I can't swim. My grandma had this friend, the wife of some low-profile mayor from a nearby tiny village. She was a nasty old bitch, but that's not our concern right now. This lady's grandson had my name. One day she visited my grandma, it was pretty early in the day, I remember I was still having breakfast. Anyway. They had coffee and all, and at one point Papio and the boys started whistling and calling my name from the street, as they were about to ride out to the river. This lady asked my grandma where the boys were taking me. She said the river. At the sound of the word river, she went bonkers. She started preaching a load of crap to my grandma in this high-pitched voice, at the speed of light, about how that river swallows people, as the currents are powerful, as there is no bottom to the river, as the military is digging in the riverbed, creating large holes and all that crap, and to remind her how her grandson died there, when he was my age, as he drowned under the eyes of his friends, and not one did anything to help him.

You know what my first thought was when I heard the story? That boy didn't have Papio with him. So shut it lady, I thought.

And so, she scared my grandma shitless, who concluded I was not allowed to go to the river anymore.

Do you think that stopped me? No way. But it did something else to me, no matter how full of BS I thought that lady was. Her story would replay in my mind whenever my feet touched water. The holes, the currents, people swallowed up. Her stupid story rearranged the way I viewed water. It was no longer a fun activity, but a life and death matter. So, there you go, that's it. From then on, I would ride with the boys, without my grandma's knowledge, but I would be afraid to enter the water.

But enough about all that, let's come back to Papio.

One morning he came to my door and said, 'This is the day. We're going in'. I was like, 'Where are we going?' He said, 'Get dressed and come down' and left.
I met him downstairs.
'The cinema just opened. The movie starts soon. We need to hurry.'
We went in through the back door, which had a strange mechanism, but Papio made a hole in the door, large enough for one of his hands to fit it, so he could work the lock. Once we were in, we went into the hall and hid behind the screen. The movie had just started and hundreds of thousands of thin needles of light penetrated the white rubber screen and were projected on the concrete wall behind it. It was as if the light was sifted through the screen, and only the story remained on the canvas, to be stared at. As we interposed between the wall and the screen, the needles were projected on our bodies and as we moved to the other side of the screen, where the ladder was, the effect created was surreal: a shower of light in the dark.
In the blue semi-darkness, we found the narrow metal ladder that led up onto a metal platform, just above the screen. We walked to the middle of the screen and looked into the cinema hall. There were about a dozen people, seduced by the screen. The soundtrack of the movie was booming all around, screams and sudden bursts of music that suggested a high-tension moment jumped off the walls of the room. We didn't linger too much and continued to the end of the platform where we found a second ladder. He started up first. This second ladder was much taller that the first and as we advanced on our climb, the light from the screen and the soundtrack began to fade. At one point Papio stepped on the ladder, indicating we reached the top. He lowered himself down towards me and said 'There's a tunnel here. It's completely dark.' He climbed all the way up to the mouth of the corridor and walked in. I did the same and followed him. By now the soundtrack of the film had vanished below us almost completely.
The hallway made a right turn, into a tighter corridor this time, even darker than before. We walked slowly, touching the walls with both hands, shuffling both our feet on the floor, so we could feel every inch of it. The one change from before was that the walls were warm, as if a fire raged on behind it. As we advanced, and slowly dragged our fingers on both walls to keep a balance in the dark, we suddenly felt them moving. It reminded me of something, but I could not put my finger on what it was. Then, from the other side of the walls, we heard a sound. In the dark, I imagined Papio turning to me, staring at me, with the same kind of panic in his eyes and heart, that stabbed mine. The sound had a rhythm. A pulse. It was pulsating. Together with the sound and the movement we noticed that the corridor began getting even tighter, and that by now it had changed its shape. It was no longer a rectangle, but a kind of tunnel of tubular shape and what we called walls felt now organic, skin-like. But the one thing we did not expect, as we carried on was the light that at end of this so-called tunnel. We initially thought it was the light of day and that we somehow managed to find an airduct or something that would lead

us out. I was ready to leave the darkness. Was Papio familiar with all of this, I wondered. As I was pondering our condition, the movement of the wall and the sound behind it synchronized, and everything around us began pulsating heavily. The tunnel became even narrower. We were now on all fours. Judging by Papio's lack of communication, I concluded that it was all new for him as well. As we got closer to the source of light, we realized that it was actually a very small door, almost square, rounded somewhat at the corners, opened towards something like a bright room.

Then Papio turned to me and said, 'This is as far as you go. You need to turn back now.' He then proceeded to squeeze through the narrow door.

The last thing he said was 'I choose to live in a story. You need to go back and tell mine.' As he disappeared in the bright room, wordless I approached the door myself and peered in. The space beyond the door was not a room, but the inside of a bus that was speeding on a highway.

As I turned to crawl out of the tunnel, the little door slam shut, and everything was dark again. I slowly made my way back to the ladder and climbed down. When I found myself behind the screen again, I decided to not walk out of the cinema, but go and find a seat and watch the movie. In the dark, I walked up a few stairs and randomly chose an empty seat. Papio's favorite film was on and as I sat there, watching the bus ride frantically with a bomb on board, a kind of fear arose in my heart – the fear of a world without Papio.

The Overwriters' Lament

David Bleiman

As Arabic superseded Greek and Aramaic as the language of
the eastern Church, the monasteries recycled their own libraries…
(Ghost Words: Reading the Past, Cambridge University Library, 2021)

day came
        fear came
and later night
        and later guilt
and took the last old greybeard monk
        for we are scrubbing smooth your skins
who'd read this Greek from left to right
        to scribe this verse from right to left
intoning the tormenting curse
        with trembling hands and heavy heads
on those who'd dare to take or tear
        across the faint and spectral past
one vellum page
        and there's the rub

The Poet's Way

Partridge Boswell

—Sheep's Head, West Cork

...wends from walled paddocks through a mute glen of sea grass curried
by ceaseless susurration gleaning secrets from a pentameter of countless
steps who've passed here one to the next... and by the time you reach

the lighthouse and peer into a tidal crevasse where three girls drowned
a century ago and so added their names to the cliffs' brutal beauty...
and see the stray lamb suckling his stray mother where the land ends

and wonder how sheep could wander so far in a shepherd's dream
and what moved people to farm such rocky desolate slopes where
wind tears at mandrake roots, and why still they try—unless perhaps

the gale's plaintive howl reminds them every moment to joyfully toss
their entire life into the scales of fate... and by the time you pass a small
shrine tucked into the cliffside—Our Lady of the Wayside—her open

arms and beatific gaze imparting succoring grace to any wayward
traveler in need of rest or strength, plodding hungrily up to the car
park's stone café to brave the tour bus crowd after communing all

day with metaphysics of wind and sea—the solitary self, a high cairn
set in stark relief against the sky... straining, reaching out to touch
what's either light in god's face or the backside of just another cliché,

before your soul can get its bearings and shrink... you leave their safe
complacent numbers behind to amble final miles on legs gone slack,
your sun- and salt-lashed face glowing transfigured by forces no mill

or pen can harness, your spirit untamable and wild as white horses
galloping across the bay... it's impossible to say where exactly,
which view among hundreds, what beauty too breathless to be held

or loss too sad to retell, what stretch of rock or dirt or bog sacrificed
itself to the gust that blew your heart open, which stile you clambered
over, meandering unmown fields of farms perennially on the edge of ruin,

trusting a well-trod thread as your head wandered aimless as a poet's cloud
            over landscapes real and imagined… fingering scales laden with the weight
of unshorn wool, turning your back on numbers and stones when the nurse

weighs you from birth until your last appointment's intake, every measuring
            up a gathering and scattering until even that staunch superstition fades
and falls away in the joyous mournful moan of your mother's selkie

voice drifting out with the tide. You toss your entire life in anyway,
            shattered and unrecognizable to anyone but you, burnished clean
of every bright path, tried or true, the fleet shadow of every thought.

Berlin 1961, 2003

Ryan Caidic

Grief is a wall dividing Mitte and Kreuzberg,
155 kilometers of palpable longing.

It is a man clawing his way through a tunnel
to go back to his wife,

a mother jumping from the third floor of her apartment
to get back to her children,

two brothers climbing through barbed wire
to live.

It is also a father from a Philippine island
bequeathing his prized collection of leather shoes

to his son, oxfords painstakingly polished,
arranged in an anachronism—Volkspolizei

parading old ideology in a new world, smelling
of vodka and cigarettes, of Berlin in the 80s. The son

politely tries them on, knowing they would never fit,
size 9 to his 13, soles that could not contain a world

in so meager a mold, striding in lofty footsteps.
So the son smiles, the way a giant

pities the man on his palm,
as a concrete rift erupts

in the spot in his chest
where a hammer used to pound, elongating

for miles, as one does when one becomes
a man himself, extending further away

into new islands, countries that are planets,
and in place of shoes,

a war, until everything becomes a sinew
of light through a crack between the bricks—flickering.

Mermaid Archipelago
Patrick Chapman

I

The night before your mother drowned
in you, her human feet
scissor-kicked with natural élan –

holding their own amongst
a Busby Berkeley shoal of
merman acrobatics on the town.

The morning after, she awoke,
having washed up on the shore
of nineteen sixty-eight.

II

Leaving what her letter called
the obsolete,
she disappeared into

some old aquarium
where they perfect
a sublime consummation

with that communal shark
of a husband
until their lips turn blue.

III

Buried in a fallen sunrise,
she would haunt the obvious rock,
and weave her seaweed hair

with dorsal fin of dragonet
and cry out to be carried home
on any passing shipwreck.

First watch

Anne Connolly

In this room we nod a recognition of our unexpected tryst with
strangers and conversation flitters on the necessary skin of life.

A book needs concentration and thinking suffocates all hope.
A spin of wheelchairs. Grim. The gape of a hungry grave.
Staff call out our name and lead us through.

We see a woman rock-a-bye a slow hypnotic beat, a low Beatles'
hum to trigger something somewhere in the swaddled bundle
that must be her man. A kiss of unrequited sound.

We reach the neatness of his bed. Not the daily tumble of charger,
earphones, iPad, cans scrunched hard as any superhero's certainty.
Only a battalion of machines that hum.

His father crumbles in slow motion, mumbles do-you-remembers?
trawled up from the forgiving hold of childhood.

My voice is drier than thirst so I touch him tender as a prayer.
Seep in his warmth. Lean close to breathe in the heave of measured
breath. Umbilical. And I think of the tingle of first milk,

the search of snuffling skin against my breast and under the anonymity
of mask I recognise his cashmere chin growing into manhood.

Hidden Dip

Eamon Cunningham

My father taught me to ride a bike,
his firm right hand gripped the saddle,
the left steadied the long handlebars
as I champed and strained to be free.

From an early age I watched him tuck
trouser legs into his long socks, push
off with firm strokes until in motion,
steady, before slinging the free leg over.

I loved the effortless way he pedalled
when I was propped on the crossbar,
arms in between his, holding on, pretending
that I was in control as the gears changed.

Those freewheeling downhills frightened
when the wind stole my breath in a hurtle
towards the dip, momentum driving us up
the opposite slope in a race for the brow.

I wanted to go it alone under my own steam,
without warning the hands slackened,
a gentle de-coupling, a singular movement
as I finally took off, leaving him in the wake.

Resident

Patrick Deeley

I am suffered by the shiny iroko hover
of this house. It is roomy enough
to keep me. I float down hallways, swivel
above landing stairwells, fade
into a drawing room wall. Untouchable,

though occurrence and absence
lose their meaning where I'm concerned.
Do you expect I search, a frown
on my face, an aura of blanched energy
cloaking me over? Am I here at all?

Am I not here? Shadow, semblance,
maybe a play on your jittery disposition?
Inside a realm of brick and glass,
lit by oil paintings, my allotted hour recurs;
I spin a cat's-cradle of hand gestures

that don't alter from one year to another.
No grief or disorder presses me
through the twilight round. I grow
neither brightened nor burdened by notions
of what may happen in the future.

Nor do I yearn to dance or dither, given
to the fluctuant open air where
a lumpy ivied pergola still arches its spine,
nor to hang by rubblework walls
echoing the gabbles of children as they

rise and fall. You won't catch me
reaching to retrieve my "psyche" or "soul"
from swallowtail, gulf fritillary
or longwing, all at home in their vivarium,
among passion vine, vanilla orchid

and jasmine. Instead, I simply happen,
a rustle, a ruse, on sprightly days
an enthusiasm of air, a glimpsed something
out of the ordinary, a whisper
slipping the noose of a silken tether,

while beyond the windows tour buses
scuddle over loose cobbles and newly-weds
are snapped smiling in the flower garden,
backed by big trees, sun or rain,
or the natural confetti of cherry blossoms.

Sizing Up

Katie Donovan

Ascending to the menswear store,
I listen to the pigeons on the roof,
their scuffles, bills and croons.

The snug fit of the jacket pleases you;
the trousers' tailored waist. Sleek and natty, unlike
your father's old suit, which is the wrong shape.

You pace towards me, testing your steps
as you once did when you were small.
At seventeen, this new ensemble

lends you a panther's prowling grace,
yet beneath the jacket's sharp lapels
beats a tender heart; above, beams a boy's face.

I hope the world will stretch you lightly,
and not to ripping point, my shining son.
That you'll have your natural span.

That love will come for you
and fold you in her arms,
when I no longer can.

You walk away.
The pigeons fall silent.
I go to pay.

Climbing the Wall

Ger Duffy

When my father tried to climb
the dining room wall, he ran at it,
pawed it, tried to pat it as if he might
find an entrance. He ran at the wall,
making climbing movements with his knees,
raising his hands to grip it. Finally, he fisted
it, we just watched him. He slid down
the wall, stayed crumpled there.
Then we let the undertakers in.

Pick a side, any side

Mark Fiddes

Sunday night between fragments of moon
scattered on a hot tide
we breaststroke out to the buoy
pillow by salt pillow
like the sea dreamed us up
from plastic bobbins and weed.
Red and white freighter lights jig
along shipping lanes and further out
the dark rigged Leviathans
of Liberia and Panama slumber.
You can taste the burn from here.
The choke of it.
The lives emptied into the swell.
A mermen's lot of boredom and rust.
Our arms clamp around the chained float.
Even with the current behind us
it is a fair way back and we saw jellyfish.
Gerry says a beer would be nice
when the airspace screams open
from across the Gulf.
Two jet fighters sweep overhead,
low and grey as doves
One beat later, the roar
that is all the world we knew and loved
being sucked into a small hole.
The waters barely stir.
Above us, only sky.
Don't worry,
I reckon they must be ours, says Gerry.
Whoever we are now.
On the beach someone is lighting a barbie.
They are playing Fontaines D.C.
Race you back, I say, kicking
the depths with the strength of a frog.

TELLING WILL

Alison Gorman

A galaxy of paper moons floats above us,
lanterns cast soft light on our entrees.
I'm guiding a pea flower dumpling

on chopsticks into my mouth, biting the carved
purple pastry, tasting a burst of peanut
and black vinegar when you ask me.

Telling you about my father is not on the menu.
A mother-son night—eating Pad See Ew,
drinking Singhas at Chon Thai.

We're talking about your work at The Pier,
how you love to pull the perfect brew,
the money you're saving at last.

I'm thinking about how much you have matured.
You don't have to tell me. Your words arrive
from another place. Rehearsed,

careful, feeling your way through the dark.
I've practised this moment too. Telling you.
Absent family always present.

On the next table, a young woman's face is lit
by a sudden blaze of birthday candles,
clustered on a coconut pandan cake.

She covers her mouth with both hands in surprise.
And I tell you about him. You listen,
walk around to my chair and hold me.

Walking Meditation with Dead Brother on his Birthday

Mary-Jane Holmes

Was it the kestrel keening for voles off the gable end that woke me
or the wind holding and releasing the roof-felt like waves hitting
a sand bank? Did I miss this morning's sunrise because the march
of cloud from the west had so much more drama, more grief?
Did I even think of the wren, its ridiculous song fifty times its weight
wrestling insects with its thin thin beak from the lichen on the wall
outside my window, or notice the curled post-it note with a faded
handwritten quote from Tembo: *I wish this body might be dew in a field
of flowers.* It's hard to ignore the state of these window frames
and the front door's rotting storm guard. Should I have considered Jesus,
who started out as a carpenter like his father and how we all for a time try
to please our parents? And the desiccating bluebottles filling the sills,
don't you think I should brandish the dustpan and brush? What if
as teenagers, we hadn't rouged our cheeks to get into that La Rochelle
nightclub (how you seduced everyone) – would we have loved life just
as it was? Are there any meadows left? Sorry, what was the question again?

Family Founding Myth

Julie Irigaray

While my father waited with his mouth
wide open for his cavity to be fixed,
the dentist was talking to my grandmother:

your son is top of the class in English.
Have you considered sending him
to England next summer?

My grandmother worked ten hours a day
in an espadrille factory, her husband was
a metalworker, they came from a line of

farmers since time immemorial, so no,
she *hadn't considered this possibility.*
But because she'd stopped going to school aged

eleven, my Grandma always trusted educated
people: the priest, the teacher, the doctor,
the dentist. It would cost two months' salary.

Back home, my Grandma used the dentist's
arguments with my grandfather: *good for*
his future   *better job opportunities.*

She sealed the deal. And so it was that
my fourteen-year-old father embarked on
a language trip to England in 1975,

leaving his village for the first time to go
abroad, and to *LONDON!*, crossing
the whole of France by train, not going to

the loo for twelve hours to avoid paying for
public toilets, taking the ferry at Calais,
crossing the English Channel, discovering

the white cliffs of Dover – the same trip
I'd undertake thirty years later. I imagine
him ogling English girls in miniskirts,

being dragged against his will to all
the tourist spots: Buckingham Palace,
the British Museum, the National Gallery.

My dad was a country boy at heart: he bought
a pair of binoculars made in USSR which he
still uses for birdwatching fifty years later.

I've been told countless times the story of
the *horrible cucumber sandwiches* his host
family made for lunch that he threw in the bin,

I've been told countless times that he was
the only working-class kid among children
of professors, lawyers, doctors, and solicitors.

I know my dad *didn't have the right to be lazy,*
that he worked hard in class and won a prize:
a biography of Shakespeare I inherited

because he's never read a book in his life.
I know he was proud to bring home this trophy
(the only book in his house was a dictionary),

and that he's still proud of having
beaten *these daddy's boys*
who didn't need to fight.

Glory Through the Clouds

Connor Johnston

I

Glory though the clouds – my grandad dies
Somewhere under a white hospital sheet.
I salute at one, then two little magpies
And feel less and less heat

In my fingers holding my phone to my ear
As I listen to my mum tell me slowly
Grandad's going to disappear
Off somewhere holy.

Glory through the clouds – visible beams
Descend on the city's dreaming spires
In a fan of butter, cloud, and cream
Mixing to a pale fire

In which our pride – his, dad's and mine –
Submits to the divine.

II

Capacious family graves collect us all
Like pieces of a set, an incomplete,
Until the surname sees to all its wards.

Unlike the graves of war, each tomb is built
Unique like rotting teeth, or marble die,
Or lilies dark with freshly ruptured dirt.

We stand there at the foot of a regret
Beneath the spears of rain that rustle worms
And thank the Spearmen that we're healthy yet.

We drown a little happiness, then leave
A fresher pair of father and the son,
Now purer than we were, more self-aware.

And our scattered thoughts resolve to just the one:
That urgency of living in the air.

III

The moon was once a shameless, brassy sun;
Her stillnesses are but the lasting dregs
Of once a life as brazen as the day

From whom the lights receded, one by one,
As quiet as an Araucana's egg,
A little luminescence tucked away.

And moons will come of suns forevermore
As long as there are suns to burn away,
For those who cannot cope yet with the day.

I stroked the soft, shorn grass until the dawn
But could not stay.

The Removal

Maeve Keane

Lying foetal on the road was the tiniest body.
Mouse or shrew, I couldn't be sure.

Crouched low, we examined the scene.
Dogs sniffed, camera clicked;

evidence to be explored later.
The pygmy shrew is common throughout Ireland.

Heading for home, I walked on, feeling
an uncanny prickle of eyes on neck.

Looking back, I saw the coroner had arrived.
One for sorrow in black and white.

Birds don't wink but I saw his eye glitter;
scarab beetle flutter-blink, green and blue.

He gently lifted the little corpse,
life and death on the glorious wing.

The catkins quivered in the hazel tree morgue.
Sparrows scattered.

Susurrus. Terminus.
Shrewd.

Sabbath Ritual

Mona Lynch

I had a father but was sometimes fatherless.
His nurturing diverted to his white collared friend in a pint glass.

Saturday nights spent drowning demons – horrors of war,
survivors' guilt. Nevertheless, he rose early on Sunday morning

to attend mass, mingle with neighbours, dance the dance.
He began his ritual with shoe polishing. Then taking his cut-throat razor

from its wooden case, he'd tug the strop dangling from its hook
by the window. With controlled rhythm stroke the razor up, tilt it

on the way down, using the ball of his thumb to check, a satisfied surgeon.
Placing it on the ridged wooden draining board,

he'd fill the rotund Toby mug with water hot from the kettle on the hob,
lather the badger-haired brush on the lump of Lifebuoy soap.

Candy floss jowls sagged under shaggy brows. Grin, scrape, grin scrape,
round the bends, skim the slopes. An equine toss in an avalanche of water –

job done.

His youngest, *his old segotia,* I'd approach eager to see the finished job,
watch the light caress his face, showing divots stuffed with blood-stained paper,

testament to a shaky hand.

Grey Rug on a Grey Field

Niamh Mac Cabe

Evening, and there's a dead horse in the field by the T-junction
someone has draped it with a heavy grey rug
it's getting dark out, I'm watching from the gate
the horse-shaped rug is becoming identical to the ground

This morning, I noted the living horse lying stretched out in the field
I noted its nostrils whorling fantastic pale creatures in the rising fog
I thought: here's an animal taking the early streaks of sun, like me
(the dawn was one of those glowing ones, the ground warm)

And don't horses sometimes do this, lay so still, so quiet
then roll sudden onto their backs like pups, I've seen them
snorting, kicking their fetlocks, pivoting on withers
rubbing wild mohawk manes into the ground

Late afternoon, a little troubled, I stand at the gate again
the sun has gone, the animal has not moved
it lies breathing, now beneath a child's colourful duvet
Buzz Lightyear, from shoulder to hindquarters

I see the horse's open mouth, the slow-roll eye
a school-scarf bunched under the large white head
To Infinity… and Beyond! arching along the spine
a young girl standing by, gesturing into her rhinestone phone

Before night falls, I walk back
the girl is gone
a stiff rug cloaks the carcass in grey
the child's duvet is beneath, tucked around the animal

I open the gate, enter the dark field

The girl's earlier footprints are here, embedded in the ground
they circle circle her horse
the imprints of her knees are at its head where she had held it
held it, at the end, until the light began to turn

A Newfoundland takes an ill-advised trip to Macroom, 1922

Bernadette McCarthy

The five of us lingered too long in Dick's Hotel
over whiskey and water. Three officers, the driver,
and myself, slumped in the musk of those who had left the bar,
of horse blood flowing from the knackery upstream.

I heard them first: urgings in the square,
and then, above the hot screech of the mart,
I smelt them—woodbines, apricot duck-shit—
and the electric fear of my master.

I barked at the glinting barrels till he bade me be quiet,
saw the lump rise in his throat like a woodcock.
The strangers saw it too, collars bristling on their necks.
I could have taken them.

On the drive west, braced together in the truck,
I pressed my snout against his burberry coat,
smelt cut bluebells from without,
laughing girls, a rotting badger in a ditch.

Note: On April 26th, 1922, four British soldiers and a Newfoundland dog were picked up by the IRA in Macroom, taken to Kilgobnet, shot, and buried in a bog.

Nowhere Shone Like Beauharnois

Kathleen McCracken

My father's father
was a farrier. From his father
trade in fire and iron, sparkfall
over troughs of river water,
maw-lure of forge-din.

Nowhere shone like Beauharnois
in autumn. The horses of Huntingdon
fitted and trimmed, abrim
with clean hooves, fresh shoes –
his handiwork an alchemy.

When it came to Vimy Ridge
he followed orders, hammered picket spikes
cold-shod, fed and watered
sluiced mud and blood
from mouths and ears and nostrils

bandaged barbed wire wounds
harnessed drafts, loaded mules
brushed and clipped, repaired and marched
flanked by hide-scent, trudge-grit –
their requisitioned obedience.

At Passchendaele refused
to despatch a shattered mare,
dappled Percheron, the one
stepped in between
to take the blast.

My father's father died at home.
Declared sleep of the just
a chimera. Around his bed
an honour guard of horses –
his breath with theirs as they

took trench-flood, mortar-fire
in stride, made high ground
north of the Laurentians,
a receding line of blue
along the western front.

The great dance of the treelike kelp

Afric McGlinchey

Storm Barra arrives as you're climbing
the *stira* to your study in the loft,
and you lift into the cosmological drama
watch as your tropical bougainvillea petals,
one by one,
are shaken off,
while the green leaves, like stars, remain steadfast

*

He comes in, shattered, collapses
All day, he's been digging down
into the newly-laid driveway, to replace
a crushed sewer pipe

*

You'd like to tell him not to let stress swallow his sleep,
that reality usually leads to some resolution
and the planet isn't going anywhere,
or at least, not this hour,
but you're not one for calmness yourself

*

You sit up in bed and listen to nature's outrage
Drink water, open the window a crack
Is the world speeding up?

You feel your breasts and panic
You think of the virus leaping from breath to breath
like a Mexican wave in a stadium
You struggle to breathe and panic

Suddenly every part of your body hints at a death sentence
You think this at 3.41am, while listening to rain
growing louder, raining like plastic
raining into bins
feel a tug where your ovaries live,

sense even the millennia-dead stars swivelling
And outside, the sea's gone out of its mind,
            and Barra shakes the walls and your bed,
like an old lover back for revenge

And at 5.44am – the storm still prowling like a wild dog –
you cave and chance Netflix

But even during the distraction of *My Octopus Teacher*
the voice of the storm enters the window and your head
and how can you argue with it?
Like a forest of kelp
                        dancing for octopods,
                                    such passion is
a seduction

*

Once a teenage soldier left a war to visit you
                        in hospital in another country,
and strummed you until you became a creature
                in the depths of the ocean
singing its song to the kelp

For weeks after, you tried to repeat the music to yourself

*

It's only now that you perceive
                        the concentricity
in each body

– living or elemental –

            as a way of seeing
the universe

The Burial of Ten-to-Two Blue

Paul McMahon

No one looks for the dead
among the dead – *that was*
the solution. So, I waited
until it got dark and when
I found the lidded-over
grave the gravediggers dug
earlier, I began digging.
Hear nothing, I told myself,
not the night-birds, not your
own breathing, nothing
till the spade hits wood.
In this silent darkness
I was a giant – the shoulder
of the spade was a rooftop,
my foot crushing it down
through eaves as the blade
pressed into the clay.

When I climbed out from
the turmeric soil, I dragged
Ten-to-Two Blue's corpse
to the edge and dropped him
onto the closed lid of the coffin
then refilled the grave and patted
the barrow down as the gravediggers had left it that morning.
Before leaving the graveside
I paused to gather my breath –
the grave-tops looked like the rooftops
of a steepled holy city, grave-crosses
rising up from a hundred churches
whose bell towers were the hilted handles
of knives, the blades driven down
into the starved ribs of cobbled streets

and as I looked over the city of the dead
I felt myself rise, exalted, a holy man
at the edge of a defeated desert,
returning to bowed disbelievers.
When I flung the spade into the gaping dark
it whirled through the captured air
like the wings of rooks in the belfry
and I walked towards the horseshoe gateway
with the great tidal hum of the universe
washing over me.

FALLEN

Audrey Molloy

Wives are afraid of me now.
They smile at me the way people smile

at leopards through glass, or across a moat:
how safe we are, over here, in our marriages.

A woman can wake to her own wailing.
How silly, they will say, *this is the sound of guilt;*

think of the children, they'll say, not hearing the plane
at work on her heart, shaving it to a leaf.

Oh, I read the Russian novels
(and you're not sure now if I mean *read* or *read*—

if this is happening or has already happened.
With loss, both can be true at once).

If the books don't lie, I die at the end of the story,
like Anna, or Emma—the fellow-fallen,

how almost *accidental* it sounds! Fallen—
as though I'd lost my footing, stumbled on the lip

of the moat, or slipped like a child's doll
over the glass fence of the enclosure.

What I know of leaving: men stride forth
with purpose, some fine new place in mind.

A wife neither falls nor leaps—she ditches
into the hands of the dark air or sea,

not caring where she comes to ground,
driven only by what she leaves behind.

There Are Things

Vicky Morris

only children remember, summoned
from the sleight of shadows, found scratching
along the dead air of night. A child's fears

incarnate, like the Chinese dragon
you saw loose in the garden, breathing fire
that lit the kitchen's dusk like a cave.

Or on another no-coins-for-the-meter
blackout night, the sink's snuffed candle flame.
The stool where you stood unable to look up

at what might be inside the window's lake
of black, the almost touch on your neck.
Breathe held, like when you'd lie between

the weight of your parents, heart racing
in time with the Clock Man who paced
back-forth, back-forth around the bed,

square body held up by the ticking
of wire legs. The waiting for him
to spring up by your head.

But still, for all that manifests in dark
corners of sight, there are things
made worse by daylight.

One time, on the hill where you'd play,
the car that pulled up. The stoic couple,
her dark glasses, cigarette. Him

asking the way in the afternoon sun,
then waving you off
with a half-swaddled gun.

The Vest

Elisabeth Murawski

For Dina Pronicheva

She is silent even when
the soldier's boot
stomps on her hand,

cracking the bones. Only
the living cry out.
Crawling away

from the pit, stealthy
as a wolf or a fox
saving herself, walks

until she drops exhausted
on her brother's
doorstep. Regrets

the boy who tagged along,
who was caught. Thinks
of the round-up,

Mama and Papa, suitcases stuffed
with documents,
jewelry, coins,

food for the trip. Beaten,
commanded to wait,
what they heard next

was not the whistle
of the train to a labor camp
but the racket

of machine guns, hideous
screams. The vest,
stiff with sand

and blood, sticks to her skin.
Her brother's wife
heats water

to soften it. Together,
they pull it off in shreds,
strip by strip.

INSTANT KARMA

Damen O'Brien

All day the maggots moved inside the skink,	pregnant
with the possibilities of life	gravid
with the snouting heads of death,	no mother
ever loved her children more,	the skin bakes
where its body fell	bread
of itself broken out for any	ovipositor
wielding predator to pierce,	no saviour
ever loved its sinners more,	the skink basks
in the adoration of saints with blind heads,	blistered
with their re-incarnative force,	the fast
crank of the karmic wheel,	that hatches
skink into a host of wasps with	angel wings
not every birth is	beautiful
not every second	coming
is a king, for those who've seen a	cow
cook in the heat, a skink's	rebirth
is a far more sacred	thing.

Visitation

Jamie O'Halloran

We looked up from our garden supper
and there she was,
moth-quiet above our heads, a barn owl,

just past moonrise. We knew her down-pale breast
and valentine face blanched against night.
In another world,
we'd have called her *ghost*
for her silent passage.

How long her flight across
our table with its guttered candles,
their coral wax pooled on cotton.
My friend whispered

Owls are an omen... finishing
the sentence by naming her husband's sister
who'd been dying already for months.

Next spring, the sister finished
her deliberate death
while my friend began hers.
If she had glimpsed Minerva in that bird,

might she have stepped
over the threshold of wisdom
rather than through death's wide door?

The Prince

Ciarán O'Rourke

Clad in gleaming,
brutal, burnished steel,

the knightly Edward,
gartered black, to Aquitaine

arrived in haste,
with hardened archers,

noble kin, and men-
at-arms (determined

to slaughter or be slain)
in breezy train and retinue,

and orderly array. Through
all the sullen winter,

later chronicles maintain,
the bright, intrepid

army moved
like a rivulet of light,

vanquishing the shadows
of indolence and spite,

extending the dominion
of the valiant and the right.

The huts of passing peasantry
were fired every night.

Amply stocked, and bustling
with undiscerning beasts,

they left
the land they travelled over

broken, disembowelled:
the valley-banks and water

seemed to quake in sudden dread,
and the flushing blossom

wizen
on the air-adoring stem,

when the regal prince
went riding

with blood upon his hem –
apportioning

his revenues
with grace among his men.

& A WOMAN

Mara Adamitz Scrupe

two plus millennia past ate a simple meal
of millet & blackberries but before the terminal
– an expiatory rube perhaps or corrective
farrago – she saw the red-shouldered hawk yearning
for flight/ return/ justice & she dozed in death as though
a walker stumbling in a high wind blown off a levee
& I couldn't pick her out of a lineup if I wanted to
though in passing her vermillion caught my eye:
leather cape & woolen garments placed aside the naked
body as frontispiece or introduction her peat-browned
skin tautly wrinkled (internal organs: brain & heart
& lungs to breath the air intact) & though I can never
do enough to keep up I keep her firmly in my mind
& if there's yet some magic in this world she's Queen
Gunnhilde dug from the muck now lying in a glass covered
saracophagus but as it happens rather early Iron Age
her body ritually pinned down with pikes & branches but time
goes on & people go on to become their different selves/ indeed
(when I was eight years old & for obvious reasons
I wanted to be a nun – extremes *extremes*
you know what I mean –) she was strangled (deep groove
proof to the neck) & dumped in a bog & I'm answering
to her agonal face marked by characteristics of sacrifice
(perhaps I have it wrong) or beatific/ shining as a saint
or conversely somehow strayed from the righteous path
as Bathsheba via Jean Bourdichon's medieval ideal: breasts
small & high/ blonde & clear-eyed with a come
hither stare/ a saving grace/ a cautionary tale & forgiveness
apparently only available in forfeiture or perhaps endurance
is a hiding place & shelter (ask me the downsides of walking
around looking like Barbie) or after all ask my lovely
fair-haired young mother holed up post-divorce in a farmhouse
surrounded by cold post-war ramblers/ ostracized but still
covertly courted by the neighborhood married men & further
truth to tell my marsh lady's wide-open eyes/ her mouth
a cracked yawn in shock terrorized I suppose

in the end   & under her sway & spell I picture
the wet places of my girlhood   & my hideout alone
in the shallows amongst the tall tufted Minnesota sedge
my bare toes mushing   the slough grass roots

Waking in the Tropics After Dreaming of Snow

Laura Jan Shore

Through the window, she-oak needles shiver
under the shimmying weight of a wagtail.

My eyelids are at half-mast, languor
after a broken night's slumber. Fruit bats in the papaya.

I feel chastised by the young magpie begging for grubs.

My body melts into my chair aware
of the Brush turkey in the banana tree demolishing fruit.

A caucus of crows dive and call.
From the tangle of mangroves—a python dangles.

What lingers is the scent of snow. A North American forest:
pine cones, blue jays, the dark velvet eyes of a doe.

Wistful as the crested pigeons cooing on my deck,
I'm missing my raucous laughs with you,

our nest under the quilts, the notes I could hit,
your baritone lilt,

how my tongue like a fish, muscled its way
along the shoals of your skin until—

silent as a heron—
you scoop me up and toss me deeper

back into the gullet
of my desires.

The last man to call me Darling

Bobbie Sparrow

On Monday I brought him peaches, he thumbed
the purple blush like a ripe kiss. Teeth tore skin
to reveal golden sinew as wet as my swallow was dry.

On Tuesday I brought langoustines, hot
butter soaked his fingers as he broke the shell,
sucked out the meat, guile shone from eyes I sought.

On Wednesday I brought a Cox's pippin, a bite
still stuck in my throat, he stroked the hollow before
devouring it to the pip, which he spat on the floor.

On Thursday I brought Black sole, he stole
the silky flesh with one easy blade, claimed
I am not full so I fed him from my breast.

On Friday I brought bone broth in porcelain,
spooned it on his tongue, his eyes closed to mine.
I saw his ribs rise and fall, thought of Adam's weakness.

On Saturday I brought filet mignon, the blood pooled
on a white plate, the flesh quick to his teeth.
I picked them clean with a Bowie knife.

On Sunday I brought a wooden bowl of cherries,
each one slit at my kitchen table; pith chewed to
the first hint of almond on my tongue then inched back in.

On Monday I sat on my empty stoop, drank a glass
of air shot through with sun, it tasted like dewdrops
on a silken cobweb, shortly after the spider had gone.

Note: When cherry pits are chewed the body creates cynanide.

Sculptor

Csilla Toldy

Sculpting away each hit gets you closer
to the soul of the stone. Chiselling between each
breath, hovering in between past and future,

each hit is shaped differently. You cannot teach
being more careful or careless. An invisible
force drives your hands, a clean-cut energy which

is a leap of faith into invincible
nothingness, ever-present and sensed,
where your whole body is a pure, humble

instrument. A pumpkin carriage condensed
and dropped you here to disappear between
two hits in the air. And you find it dispensed

in space, let go and fall again, unseen.
A flash of light – a wingless flight of confidence.
The second before, what could it mean,

without the weight of its consequence
in the second after? Steadily thumping
like your heartbeat, the renaissance of eloquence,

searching the tongue, the language. Diminishing
the rock, or giving back, trying to redress.
The hands are blind, the eyes clumsy at seeing.

The core guides, hearing the light, shedding darkness.

Paper Moon

Fiona Tracey

How long have I been mourning
old versions of myself, phases already

in the ground? Tracing my face
in photographs, missing this

roundness, that hollow. Marking myself
with ink and metal, aching for scars

that were mine to choose. How long
have I been a foreigner here, marooned

in my own body, refusing
to call it home? Shapeshift long enough

and you forget your true form. Call
yourself luminous and the world

believes it. Thrown out of the underworld, I rise
like a weightless lantern, a paper moon.

Tune-up

J.S. Westbrook

We found common ground in a broken language.
He'd been around the Bloc as a mechanic
and trained, as it turned out, where I now worked.
The temple, the tower, the corniche, the ancient shoreline

he signaled with the wave of a cigarette's ember –
its power to delimit and remember,
a haven from the tides of disassembly
and displacement. Home was no consolation,

never closer than a song on the radio.
Decades of diesel fumes and tobacco smoke
had tuned his throat's low hum to a plaintive mode.
From what the meter read to what I owed

stood wastes of association, flaring gas
against the chill of night. How could I help
but warm the hands my knocking heart extended
over old flames seeping from the tenderness

with which he swung the steering wheel and ventured
through the curtains of his cataracts?
And are the girls still beautiful? Do they
still wear their hair in twin braids down their backs?

Notes from a Room
Ruby Eastwood

1. When mould started growing on my ceiling, I waited for it to spread. At first it was a small speckled patch surrounded by dampness where the paint had blistered and yellowed. Soon the separate specks merged into one. It was almost moving, like watching from above as the tide pulls away to reveal one connected landmass. It is a whole continent now, with areas of mountainous greenery. I will write to my landlord.
2. I do not usually smoke, but at the bar I take a cigarette break every fifteen minutes. I go out through the back door by the bins and smoke luxuriously under the fire escape. Sometimes the kitchen porter comes out for a cigarette in his overalls, flirting so gently it almost slips by as brotherly. We stand there smoking and flirting until the manager or the cook calls us back in.
3. Valerie Solanas advises employees all over the world to 'unwork', a process that involves deliberately underperforming, not charging for merchandise, and being on the lookout for ways to damage company equipment. 'SCUM will become members of the unwork force, the fuck-up force; they will get jobs of various kinds and unwork... SCUM will unwork at a job until fired, then get a new job to unwork at.' I wish I was uncompromising like Valerie, but I know that this job is not meaningfully worse than any other, so though I will push it as far as I can, I won't do any real damage. At the end of the month I have rent to pay.
4. I finally write to my landlord about the mould, building the case for a reduction. I attach photographs and links to related diseases: *bronchopulmonary aspergillosis, allergic alveolitis, asphyxiation.* I invent symptoms and explain them in disgusting detail, making sure to strain my syntax, as if the rot has reached my brain. It doesn't work. Instead, he tells me he will send someone in to inspect it.
5. When I first started working at the bar my manager warned me that it would get crazy around Christmas and I laughed internally at the idea I would still be here at Christmas. But having sent my CV to a number of art galleries and received no response, having tried to sell my body on the internet and found no takers, here

I am at the beginning of the new year, my hands burning as I stack hot glasses from the dishwasher in rows along the shelves. I ring the last orders bell. The drunks around me exacerbate my misanthropy, but at closing time when they are all gone and I am clearing up I feel more tenderly towards them. The objects keep their shape. There is the bright pink lipstick on the rim of the wineglass on table 13, where the nervous woman sat across from the fat man. There is the napkin that she twisted in her hands, slowly unfurling next to his empty pint. There is the damp patch where the old man sat at the stool by the bar. The beer bottles stacked in the shape of a pyramid on the counter where my manager, recently divorced, kept inviting strangers for a drink, saying 'fuck it'. He had spilled beer down his shirt and it was clinging to his skin, so you could see the pink of his flesh through the white fabric. Broken glass on the floor. By the doorway, someone's number written on a piece of paper, trodden and muddied.

If you let yourself get sentimental about small things like this, all the human misery in the world rushes in on you like water through the hole of a ship and you sink utterly. Before you know it you're weeping for the man on the corner of Talbot Street who jeers at every girl who walks past, weeping for him and the multitudes like him. So you harden yourself against it, because there's no point feeling miserable when you don't have to. And when you hear that his body, or maybe someone else's, was found frozen on a bench by the Liffey one winter morning not too long ago, you are hardly surprised. You accept it because he has done it to himself, and because you are not him, though one day you might be.

6. The sound of the traffic outside passes through my dreams, becomes the sound of the sea. When I stand up to close the window it takes a few seconds to reattach the sound to the sight of the cars on the street below. Sometimes whole days will go by like this, the reality slightly out of sync, lagging behind the dream. I will have long conversations where I appear to be listening, smiling and even responding. But I have no idea what has been said. I am somewhere else.

7. Pearl-grey light over the Liffey, white gulls. The rain has frozen in rivulets on the side of the street. Shattered glass and frost on the pavement, a siren sounding in the distance.

8. One of your best qualities was your hatred of Patti Smith. You thought she was a total sellout, a prime example of how the countercultural is absorbed into the main, of how art passes into aesthetic, loses any meaning except as a signifier of good taste among the elite. I told all my friends about this. 'She thinks Patti Smith

is lame', I said proudly. From the moment we met we entered into a wordless pact to merge into one, to scorn all others. When you were brutal about people it was funny and sexy. It affirmed their distance from us, our closeness to each other. I liked that levelling quality of your gaze when it looked on others; less when I felt it start to turn on me. Moth-like, drawn to the thing that burns me.

9. Maybe I am like all those women who like married men, I choose relationships with programmed obsolescence as a mode of self-preservation.

10. Walking through the city, threading in and out of other people's dreams. A hint of cigarette smoke from the man in a suit disappearing around the corner of Friar Avenue, cumin and cinnamon and black pepper from the Syrian restaurant on Camden Street. On days like this the scenes from all the lives I haven't lived take on a new reality; they crowd in like memories. A ship parting through the mist on the Charles river, mosaics, skyscrapers, white honey, saffron and silk. I have the urge to set out to sea. I will turn my face to the wind. I will drive down endless highways. No matter that I have no car, no licence. I will be free.

11. Went to get a new notebook and spent a long time looking through them, eventually deciding on a small black leather-bound Moleskine with a purple ribbon place marker. As I left the alarms went off and I had to run. How demeaning. Note to self: security protection can be invisible under packaging.

12. A woman in a dark blue blazer came to inspect the mould. She took pictures, zooming into the green fur, then she made a long call, describing its colour and texture. The next day a man in paint-splattered trousers knocked on the door to examine it, coming in and out of my room to stare up. The following week there was a different man harnessed outside my window with a toolbelt. For two days, he hammered and scraped. Finally, a third man came in with a small ladder and a surgical mask. He positioned the ladder, put on his mask, climbed up a few steps, wiped the mould with a cloth and then went away. None of them have come back but the mould has.

13. Penicillin was discovered in mould, if I recall. This saved many lives, changed society and earned Fleming a Nobel. Something might yet come of it.

14. Whatever I try to write ends back in this room. I am a monkey drawing the bars of its own cage. Art is meant to transcend, to redeem. I want to write scenes of magical realism, where the walls fall away or become translucent like the flesh of a jellyfish, and my room floats over the bright city. I want to write scenes with you in them, and a big moon. Scenes where we float together over rooftops, follow the

bends of the river. But I am bound by gravity, confined to talk about your absence and about the rot spreading outwards from the corner of the ceiling like a stain.

15. Once, sheltering from a downpour, we ran into the Hugh Lane. We walked around looking at the Francis Bacon paintings. I liked his room, its mess and filth. How the walls seemed to close in. It is nice to peer in through the glass panel and know you can leave. Every dirty rag, dusty newspaper image and paint splatter exactly as he left it when he died. The atmosphere of his room gets into his paintings. Airless and dank, all mottled flesh and invisible terror. 'I feel at home here in this chaos,' he said. 'Chaos suggests images to me.'

16. You asked me once what I am afraid of and I gave an evasive answer, something about the passage of time. My fear is more specific. To have spent so many years thinking I was Jean Genet only to wake up one day and find that not only have my looks vanished and I have made no valuable contribution to art, but I am too broke to buy myself a coffee.

17. It is true that I dread the stultifying comforts of bourgeois life. But I don't know how much of that dread is an attempt to make peace with inexorable poverty, to claim it as a choice.

18. Outside my window, on the wall of the building opposite, there are peeling posters for concerts, stickers and old graffiti. For a long time there was a large sketch of a naked woman, with no head or limbs, only enormous round breasts, nipples, belly button and cunt. Someone has come in the night and spray painted a bikini over her in a different colour. Is it sweet that this second round of vandals have made an effort to give her some privacy, or is it alarming that they have nothing more urgent to do than censor images of public nudity?

19. When I am paranoid everybody who gets onto the train looks like a ticket inspector. So many dark synthetic suits, so many hideous collared shirts.

20. Looked at a Rothko, pink on red. Looked at a Neel, New York rooftops in the snow. Some boring paintings of grids. Still lives, even worse. A Le Brocquy, a few Picassos. Only felt moved by the girl in the room with the abstract expressionists who looked a bit like you. Same elegance, same darkness and pallour. Something about the set of the mouth. She wore chestnut brown cowboy boots and they clicked loudly on the marble floors. Wooden heels, warm polished leather. If only great art inspired a fraction of the genuine feeling that her boots did, but I am not high minded. Art is useless to me but I can't help feeling everything might be different if I found a pair of boots like hers.

21. Do you remember that party in D4? A boy you knew invited us, his parents were away and we all took pills in what he called *the playroom*. It drove home the fact that for rich people childhood is not a cage to be fled as soon as possible but a haven, to be prolonged indefinitely, sometimes a whole lifetime. He was an awful boy, talking about Jameson and Fisher, gurning like a fool. If a real working class person talked to him you just knew he would've died. His drugs didn't kick in for a long time but we got out as we were coming up, ran to the park near his house and climbed over the metal railings. The pills made us angelic. We lay on the grass in our long coats talking and listening to music and watching the dark branches swaying above. We confessed our love for each other, we vowed it would never end. Our vision was all shuddering and star-spangled. Then on the bus back we sat the whole way in silence, still holding hands but unable to think of a single thing to say to each other.
22. I read that each time a memory is retrieved it disintegrates a little bit, like artefacts in museums that are too precious to be displayed, will crumble if exposed to the light.
23. Every night crowds rush over the bridge into the crooked streets in Temple Bar, the bright pubs with loud music. The party is long dead but every night there is dancing. Different faces with the same slack look, glazed eyes. Crowding around the McDonalds before dawn for scraps. Seagulls circling.
24. Addiction is the girl in the story with the red shoes who likes dancing too much, so her shoes are cursed to dance forever. Even after she cuts her feet off and is walking around on bloody stumps, the shoes follow her around, still dancing. In some versions of the story, the little girl dies and is taken to a place where nobody mentions the red shoes. It is unclear if this is heaven.
25. I have gladly taken the baton you handed me and I sneer at Patti Smith every chance I get. I follow her on Instagram and look at pictures of her garden, a cocktail in a dark hotel lobby, parties at the Met, cathedrals in France. All her images are captioned with short poems; they all begin the same.

*

This is
night writing
a rare cocktail
and the moon.

*

This is
where
I am.
Naples.
Where coffee
is holy.

*

This is
me
looking in at
your life
from my
mouldy room.

*

26. My manager has not slowed down since New Year's, seems to be throwing all his money at the bar, which would be alright if he owned it. He keeps buying rounds for strangers. The dutiful ones sit around while he talks about his wife, soon to be ex-wife, and some of them stay until closing, getting plied with free drinks. Most drink up quickly and go, and a few of the more shameless take their drink with them immediately.

27. Life is unfixed. It is liquid, and we are swirled around in it. Over time it hardens, leaving us stranded far away from each other with no way to get back.

28. Lying on my bed, looking up at the ceiling, I note a new development. The continent of mould is being populated. Little filaments with rounded caps are sprouting out of the fur. They look like stick people with bobble heads. Seeing as there will be no reduction to my rent, all I can hope is that the mushrooms grow into something edible that might get me through the winter. I will make risotto.

The Sea View
Lucy Holme

In 2010, the tiny, super-rich enclave of Monte Carlo was ablaze with gossip concerning former Olympic swimmer Charlene Wittstock, better known as Princess Charlene of Monaco, and how she had reputedly tried to flee the principality again. This was not the first time she had attempted to escape, the press reported, stating that she had tried three times before in the run up to her wedding to Prince Albert, the head of the house of Grimaldi and reigning prince of Monaco. On this occasion, she took refuge in the South African Embassy in Paris, and it was said she had purchased a one-way ticket back home, but her plans were thwarted and she instead returned to Monte-Carlo and the two day fairytale nuptials.

Like her late mother-in-law, Hollywood actress Grace Kelly, Charlene embraced the role of girlfriend, fiancée, and future companion of a monarch with aplomb. She learned the rules and adopted the conventions of the second smallest country in the world, a cypress-fringed 2.2 km squared jewel, nestling between Italy and France. A place so wealthy it is said to be home to roughly 12,261 millionaires in less than one square mile alone. She abandoned her former swimming life. She would now swim only in the pool designed by Grace at the Prince's Palace of Monaco on the rocky promontory of Le Rocher, overlooking the port. Somewhere in the living suites of the Palace, a portrait of Grace Kelly still hangs on royal blue walls.

When I lived in Monaco, in the early years of the 2000s, before Albert met Charlene and many years after Grace Kelly died in a car accident on the cliff road known as the *Moyenne Corniche* near La Turbie, I wondered at the mysteries inherent in this place. The cavernous gap between the Monegasques who worked and served people and those privileged expatriates who shopped, ate, and luxuriated in the pleasure of the bergamot-scented breeze was vast and undeniable. Working on one of the largest private motor yachts in the port, I was well used to secrecy, and to drama. One night, I got the call on late duty. The slow, easy drawl of my cabin mate beseeching me, 'You need to come. Get here now, please. I need you!' I had received this urgent summons from Eliza before and was often called upon to pull her out of these situations she found herself in. As usual, I felt the mix of envy coupled with genuine concern that this time she might really be in danger.

I'll admit to irritation that her adventures were always so exciting and unrehearsed. I stocked the fridges, spooning *Bonne Maman* raspberry jam into tiny petri dishes, and preparing the butter portions just the way the owners liked it (shaped into little custard-yellow iced gem swirls). I worked methodically and folded the corners of white linen lotus flower napkins stiff with starch into their ornate silver bread baskets. There were duties to work through and to tick off and I followed our checklist with the fervour of a devout church group leader adhering to Bible scripture, ensuring everything was restored to pristine and immaculate order for the morning. I refused to rush, concerned only with reaching an almost holy level of preparedness and appearing beyond reproach. Still, it was a given that I would go to her when I was done.

As I walked down the dock, I untucked my shirt and lit a Marlboro Light. The cigarette was stolen from the stash we kept on board to place on the expensive sharkskin and onyx surfaces, each packet sliced open neatly with one cigarette positioned extending out, like a slim and elegant finger. I turned left at the Stade Nautique Rainier and as I reached Rascasse corner, the driver of a forest green Bentley Continental rolled down the tinted window to greet me. As I climbed in Eliza called again to check I had met him and said she'd see me there. Her hollow tone reverberated on the line, and I heard the low, mesmeric beat of Tomcraft's *Loneliness.* It was the song of our summer. We played it on a loop in a cabriolet rental car we took to Juan-Les-Pins on the weekends. She in the passenger seat with a headscarf and enormous glasses, pale arms twirling, casting shadows on the cream interior, me following the snaking traffic on the base *corniche,* eyes darting to the anchor lights scattered across the bays. That evening however, I was not in the party mood and did not feel like making small talk with the chauffeur, Benoît, an audacious Tunisian we knew from Cap D'Ail heliport pickups. I slunk into my seat, watching the sprinklers rising and falling on manicured flower beds as the car crept slowly out of the port.

Monte-Carlo is for the rich, and for those who like to study them. Voyeurs and hangers-on wait for glimpses of socialites and obscure minor royals and for the chance to corner an ageing film star in Jimmy'z and get them braying about their infinity pools and temperature controlled glass-ceilinged wine cellars in the Japanese garden while they drink their VIP table dry. You brush against them in darkened hotel bars, inhale the genes, watch them walk into the restaurants, blasé, inflated with centuries-old private trust braggadocio and shouldering complicated family feuds, awash with European money and a dedication to decadence flowing through their veins.

The smooth faces and trans-seasonal style of the uber-wealthy was a uniform easy to spot. Designer perspex heels, Hervé Léger bandage dresses and fur boleros for the women, strapped up tight like thin, pinched, high-class table dancers. For the men, slim-cut chinos in eye-watering tones of ripe banana and teal, satsuma and bright emerald, their soft pedicured feet encased in baby blue Tod's driving shoes even though they all have drivers and never walk. The capital H glint of an Hermès belt on show and a Loro Piana cashmere jumper slung around their shoulders for when it gets cool up at Château Eza.

Nonchalant non-stares, impassive features. If by accident sometimes they glanced at you, you didn't register. They're not looking at you. You are not of their world.

Eliza moved with ease through the miniature kingdom. At public-school, she had grown up with men earmarked as leaders since the day their tearful mothers dropped them off at orientation, clad in grey flannel shorts and jackets with red piping and gold stitched crests. She had a transatlantic accent that suggested Swiss finishing school but originated in South-East England. She had learned how to climb and how to adapt, and as Monaco was the natural home of the socially shape-shifting, she blended in seamlessly.

Her usual comfort outfit, a rugby shirt with stiff white collar turned up, hands tucked inside the sleeves, was girlish and vulnerable but belied a tough core. Back then, as one of only a handful of sixth form girls in her private day school, she had let the popular boys hurt and belitte her, and had felt obliged to be grateful for their attention. Now she did whatever she wanted, whenever the impulse took hold. She was once again somewhere new and foreign with people I hadn't met, probably about half an hour away from blackout. I didn't know if she would be a match for them, or if she would come out of this one unscathed.

I inhaled leather and eucalyptus and lay back against the head-rest, weary from work. We cruised through the Fontvieille tunnel and towards Cap D'Ail and although I did not recognise the address of the residence, this wasn't strange to me.

'Some posh boys are having a party here tonight, I reckon,' Benoît said in his accented English, catching my eye in the rearview mirror. 'What is she up to? You wanna call me later? We can go to Nice if you get tired of this crowd. I've got a pick up, then I'm off at I a.m.' I shot him a look.

'Never again,' I muttered. 'I had to hitch-hike along the *moyenne corniche* at 5 a.m. to get home the last time! She left me and went to Cannes, remember?' Benoît had forgotten that occasion. He shook his head at the memory.

'She's lucky I caught her tonight, leaving the Rascasse. I followed her up here. You sure?'

'I'm good, thanks.' I said, picturing her dancing, oblivious and dreamy, in the early evening crowd before the party moved on towards the beach.

'I can wait for you both...' He hesitated. There was a community between the yacht crew and the waiters, bartenders, security, chauffeurs, and florists we got to know over time living in the principality. My favourite mornings were leaving the boat early, before the guests were awake and walking to the flower market at La Condamine on La Place D'Armes. On a few occasions, I drank espresso and freshly squeezed orange juice there with Benoît and Henri, another personal chauffeur. Shivering from the day's first weak sun rays in my uniform, usually covered in flaky croissant crumbs, I laughed at their stories, my arms crammed full of pungent lilies and opalescent roses in early bloom.

Through their stories I could imagine their hometowns and the faces of their mothers, wives and small children who waited for them to return from never-ending summers of work. It seemed we were all waiting for something to happen. On standby most of the time, our family back home celebrated birthdays and passed exams, shopped and cooked for each other, while we were paid to take the utmost care of the adults who rarely contemplated our tangled interior lives.

'I don't need rescuing, Benny,' I told him. 'But we are on warning after Cannes, so I have to get her back.' I jumped out of the car and watched as it reversed away. We had the confidence of the outsider living in Monte Carlo. We knew how to behave, so we did not show any outward discomfort. Most of the people we met at parties or clubs here were unlikely to bother with us other than just for unconditional fun. I felt sure I was safe, but wondered if I could even detect any hidden peril anymore. Following the ocean path, I looked down and saw I had forgotten to remove my sensible interior crew shoes. Without the Ferragamo scarves which identified the yacht, my black skirt and blouse rendered me dowdy, not chic. Worse, a *worker.* My uniform was passable, even elegant, onboard, but out of place in Monaco's exclusive tree-lined suburbs.

Juniper in the air and pine needles crunching softly underfoot, I eventually came upon the perfect vista and saw her there almost at once, sitting on the edge of the sunset. Writers have tried with varying degrees of success to render the curious luminosity of that stretch of the Riviera coast. The gaudy opulence contrasted with a shadowy shingle underbelly has riveted writers from F. Scott Fitzgerald and Edith Wharton to Graham Greene and Somerset Maugham who have strived to describe its allure. The cool incense of the night, its waves of jasmine and the scent of the sea was hypnotic and I could understand how Eliza was always drawn back into the darker elements of what the night had to offer.

Her black hair was an inky cloud and the party, all around her, was reflected on her face and in the eyes of strangers stretching into the house with its glass balcony and white shutter boards. A sky to ocean floor expanse of blue-gold turquoise shone, canvas-like, with a few small sailboats anchored in the bay their pin-prick masts swaying. In the sky, a handful of bright polished stars winked as if to welcome us to this scene we had no business with, this dangerous place with its perfect view of Plage Mala, a lavender garrigue seascape that was every person's Condé Nast beach house fantasy.

Our life together as friends and cabin mates ran through my head. I thought of all the Menthol Vogues we had smoked on the dock, chased down with champagne. Of us in Gucci florals and velvet platforms at the Columbus Hotel. Our attire paid for from envelopes stuffed with tips and far too elegant and grown-up for our nocturnal activities. The weekends driving from Cap D'Ail to Cannes in a rusty brown car we had bought for €100 from another yachtie, the keys of which we then raffled to a sail boat crew in a trunk bonanza pre-Caribbean season dock party. Nights spent stealing hand towels and souvenirs from marble restrooms in a Beausoleil pied-à-terre, simultaneously pressing the buzzers of all the neighbours in the building, breathing in the sanatorium-sterile smell of the unblemished corridors.

The place was an immaculate haven of manufactured perfection. No litter, no riff-raff allowed. We learned how to act aloof as unofficial guests of honour at the midnight swimming pool parties that took place shrouded from view. Royals in symmetrical formation gazed down in gilded frames, from the wall of every shop, every café and apartment but every night bad behaviour dominated. People say things became calmer in the province after Albert married Charlene. The shaky fairytale had been allowed to continue. This year there were rumours he promised to pay her €10,000,000 a year to return to fulfil her royal duties after health issues had taken her out of the principality. A figure, and concept, disputed by the palace.

I had, over time, invented my own fairytale, my own reasons for staying. The idea that I could transcend this servitude, my relegation to the fringes of this society of which I had somehow become a member and figure out my purpose was intoxicating and for a time, it felt within our reach. Two months earlier, I had almost become the steady girlfriend of Daniel, a man whose start-up success story was a Premium Rate Services company. Intensely proud of his 5 digit short codes (the least glamorous of start-ups imaginable) he found himself, after a speedy accumulation of wealth, with a Monte Carlo mezzanine flat and a driver, looking for someone to talk to at night that reminded him of home.

One weekend he took me to St Tropez by speedboat. A roaming silver fox photographer with an SLR took photos of me perched on Daniel's knee in Cinquante-Cinq after too many Domaine Ott magnums at lunch. I was awkward and unfunny in front of his work colleagues and their smiling fiancées, a roll call of Tatler society princesses. He put his arm around me when I got so tired and drunk I couldn't face the journey back. 'Let's stay longer,' he pleaded, giving me a little squeeze. 'We can take the helicopter back later on.'

I pretended to have watch duties early the next day so I wouldn't have to stay with him. Although I didn't want to kiss him, I did, anyway. I hadn't paid anything towards lunch and besides; I wondered if I should consider him a realistic prospect. I tried to quash the onset of boredom, concentrating on the filmy soft-focus image of dating and then potentially marrying for money. I thought of Madam, married for thirty years to the owner of the yacht I worked onboard. His boat, never hers. Despite the fact she had chosen each fabric swatch and every piece of silverware. Of how, as the yacht tender departed for the heliport with her and the children after a family holiday, another speedboat would be incoming with his girlfriend Amandine and a few of her twenty-something friends or another glamorous escort he met in London or Paris and was trying out for the weekend. I was forever removing silk panels and storing personal items in the secret cupboards. I thought of the time spent removing long hairs of different expensively dyed hues from silk pillow cases and bleaching foundation-stained white waffle facecloths.

I pictured myself in ten years' time, in jodhpurs and a Barbour jacket loading dogs into the boot of Daniel's Land Rover. Two bilingual children strapped into the backseats with straw boater hats and those ubiquitous blazers with crests. I wondered what that would be like. A life in this shiny prison knocking back champagne in the laps of wealthy hedge funders or, perhaps, export back to the Gloucestershire countryside to tend rose bushes and design charity luncheon seating plans. Were there other options than the ones presented to me? Not within the company I was keeping. I didn't know yet where I was expected to end up, and living here was only further warping my sensibility.

When Eliza and I were drinking shots of sambuca in the Rascasse and Daniel walked in late, looking for me, I always scanned the room first to see if there was someone better connected or more fun, before finally relenting and talking to him. From one or two dates, I conjured a mistaken lifetime from which I could not extricate myself. When I thought of how he was one of the few earnest and genuine people I had met during my time there, I felt guilty. I was not above judgement for the ways in which I had begun to scheme and lose the grip of my own shaky moral compass.

It soon became clear that Eliza needed help. I could usually judge the depth of the cocaine and Cristal haze she was likely to be in and how much assistance we would require. That night, I detected a new blankness in her eyes. I looked around and recognised the usual crowd of yacht brokers and investment bankers with chic European minor celebrities for companions and then there she was staggering towards me, drink in hand, sloshing champagne over the sisal rugs.

I grabbed the arm of a yacht broker from Chelsea that we knew well. 'What did you give her? For God's sake! It's not the weekend for us! The boss is at the hotel with clients tonight.' Jonathan merely shrugged and attempted to put his arms around me. I pushed him off roughly. This evening's client (the boss's mistress, Amandine) was twenty-five, barely older than I was. I had unpacked her clothes and lingerie when she arrived this morning and I would fold each item painstakingly back into tissue paper and into her monogrammed luggage when I packed for her departure, which would probably be at 4 a.m. on Sunday after a prolonged screaming argument with the boss.

Despite her position and wealth, life was no easier for Amandine. The path she had followed to becoming the compliant and mostly silent mistress of a man of questionable business dealings might have begun with an evening much like this one. A sideways look, then dancing; the potent feeling of being swept up in something astonishing. Now she was one of a long list of companions, marginally higher up the scale than some of her counterparts due, in part, to youth and novelty value.

We had all, on occasion, wriggled out of uncomfortable corners and backed away from wealthy men after they had consumed too much tequila or whiskey, taking up all of our air and breathing down our necks on the jacuzzi decks as we tried to clear canapés or fix cushions. We were all as disposable and replaceable as each other. What salaries we pocketed and how we might one day use that financial freedom to fuel our individual dreams were our own business.

Eliza and I had no social currency there, no friends in that villa with its incredible views of a glistening, fathomless sea. I had no way of knowing which little pill or wrap had caused these side effects, and I understood there was no one to help us. Our families were in England, we couldn't call the police. Our friends were all in transit. We were stateless and nomadic in the eyes of Monaco law, living in a place where you would be arrested for vagrancy if you were found drunk by the escalators outside Carrefour in Fontvieille with less than €50 in your pocket.

Our boss was at Le Louis XV at the Hôtel de Paris at this moment with Amandine. He would be back soon, and if I was not standing there on the aft deck when he returned, with a tumbler of Russian Standard vodka on a tray and an arm extended to light his Montecristo cigar I would be fired.

We existed half between two worlds with no-one to miss us should we fall. I realised that all my energy had been spent emulating these lifestyles while freeze-framing my own progress. Throughout the past year I had been stashing away the Euros I earned in order to live an expensive-looking life whilst shopping for €2000 Christofle ashtrays for the boss's wife and fielding advances from his creepy married sexagenarian friends. In the meantime, all the fun had become fraught. These people didn't care about Eliza, how funny she was. They didn't know how fiercely protective she was of her Law & Order DVD box sets or about her penchant for a mug of Bisto when she was hungover. They did not know what we had been through together. As much as she needed me to bring her back, I wanted to return us to our safe existence, to our rectangular little cabins, our repetitive duties and endless lists.

I took her drink and then her hand. She was half crawling on the white-painted floorboards. She looked at me, desperate and suddenly empty. All the party drained from her. At that moment, I felt a protective pull towards this strange friend with whom I had been thrown together, coupled with overwhelming anger for yet another responsibility from which I had to absolve her. But who was good for me? Who I should surround myself with? Nothing fitted. 'This is the last time, I promise,' she croaked, her grey saucer eyes fixed on me.

'C'mon, let's get out of here,' I said. It wouldn't be the last time and she wouldn't remember all of this tomorrow, but it didn't seem to matter anymore. Tomorrow she would not recall the chaos or the shock of seeing her pale face and jagged movements. I would once again be cast in the role of the prim, pinched person, reminding her of her indiscretions, but at least she would be safe. We found her bag and shoes and I threw her arm around my neck and pushed her out of the villa and up the hill, to the coast road.

While the urge in her to self-destruct was always present, it loomed large and unwieldy that night. Like the bloated moon and the vast expanse of the Mediterranean Sea, it had an endlessness and inevitability to it. I thought of when the painter Francis Bacon once said of Monaco and its environs, 'I love being on this coast. With this light, one always seems to be on the edge of the real mystery.' I saw how the story might have unfolded from that vast picture window and imagined us as tiny droplets in the sea, invisible to the naked eye. We were often invisible unless needed to procure something seemingly essential or to massage a guest's fragile ego, only then did our shapes take on a more useful form. All I could hold onto was that everything would be different and somehow cleaner in the daylight. That was the sole truth available to us.

I decided then that she and I would not end up ashore without a trace, forever emblematic of the dark side of this glittering state. We would see this view again—a different apartment, another night—and I would be there to take her hand and walk her out into the morning, to make sure she didn't disappear completely.

We had seen too many women lost and irrevocably changed by wealth, by loneliness and isolation. I harboured hope that we might still be about to forge our own path, and navigate our way together out of the shadows cast by this chimerical existence, but for now we would return to our home in the principality, to our corresponding roles. To fulfil what was expected of us.

The Winter of the Straw Bale Furnace
Johanna St John

Winter in Denmark is a black curtain. A tentative cloud of daylight exists only at the height of the afternoon. Everything else is darkness and, during that year, snow, snow, snow. In 2010, Bornholm came face to face with its worst winter in half a century, and this just happened to be the year we lived there on that tiny Danish island, a white-frosted parallelogram floating in the Baltic Sea.

Mornings were ink-black and icy, streaked with wind that froze blood and numbed fingers. Their heaviness embodied the weight of that winter and everything that had led up to it. Nothing had happened the way it was supposed to happen.

My mother, burdened with our situation, woke long before dawn to make mornings bearable. An hour before I had to be up for school, she plucked herself from her cocoon of quilts, pulled on heavy-duty boots, and braved the outdoors to start up the straw bale furnace. Its fire warmed the water that trickled through the ancient heaters in our house. Hulking in one of the barns, the monstrous smoke-blackened machine filled a whole room. My mother—Mor, in our household Danish—refilled it every few hours to keep us warm. The furnace door clanked and wailed as it swung open, the organs of straw behind it reduced to crackling coals in their metal cavern. Mor used a pitchfork to fill the yawning furnace to the brim once more. Flames licked the straw bales and smoke billowed around her before she closed the door with a thud. She came back wearing a perfume of ash.

Until that year we'd only spent summers at the two century-old farmhouse, which my parents owned to give their children some sense of belonging, *somewhere*. My dad's job at the UN relocated us every few years, but our house in Denmark provided structure to our otherwise unpredictable placement in the world. As a summer house, it lacked any modern central heating. In preparation for that winter, my mother, sisters, and I had spent several autumn days dragging straw bales on tarps across the courtyard to stack them in the furnace room. I felt strangely excited about this eccentric chore, as if I knew we were gathering stories we'd tell for the rest of our lives.

We took turns sawing firewood, too, keeping logs in the kitchen's woodstove ablaze and letting them sink to hot embers as we slept. I was twelve years old and sawed firewood blasting a middle schooler's dream playlist in my ears: Mika, Owl City, Bieber, Maroon 5. I watched my breath appear in puffs, spurred by the prospect of cinnamon-spiced hot cocoa and chocolate chip cookies fresh from the oven. We probably made several thousand chocolate chip cookies that year; they were our specialty.

In the 5:30 AM fog, when it was time to get up for school, Mor opened my bedroom door and sang, "Johaaanna." I can still hear her voice, carrying me on a fluffy white cloud from my dreams.

The stones I'd warmed on the woodstove and buried at the foot of my bed were now cold and damp. I nudged them away with my toe and tried to deny the prospect of morning by coiling myself under the blanket sanctuary.

"Johaaaaanna."

I could smell fresh bread: my favorite scent, quintessentially Bornholm. I associated it with complete family breakfasts. The six of us surrounding a steaming loaf, Mor and Dad disagreeing about how to slice it.

When I'd torn myself from the covers, I spread margarine and honey over hot slices of bread and ate them while doing what I'd learned to do from my new Danish friends: straightened my hair, applied eyeliner, and paired fuzzy socks with leggings. My mother, involuntary night owl running on three hours of sleep, stayed up to keep me company. She sat in her favorite armchair, working on handicrafts in a soft pink bathrobe worn thin at the elbows.

Not even a hint of morning light had appeared in the sky when the time came for me to catch the bus. I armed myself against the cold with a hat, scarf, and gloves my mother had knitted for me during the fall. Smokey, our beloved cat—given his unimaginative name ten years prior by my sister—lay curled on the couch. His fur, polished charcoal, rose and fell as he breathed whatever dreams consume feline sleep. I felt intensely jealous of Smokey and Snowball, our other old cat, as they slumbered to their heart's content. Nothing to pull them from sleep, nothing to drag them out into the cold. I longed to be a cat.

Snow had fallen thick and unstoppable for a week, which on an island of dirt roads and unpredictable buses meant days without school. But the snow ploughs had finally made it out, growling like monsters as their lights flashed across our neighbor's barren cornfields in the night. Wherever they couldn't penetrate, the snow had become so compacted you could walk on top of it as if on a frozen lake. Our stretch of country road was elevated with a meter of snow that didn't budge beneath my feet, and I clambered on top of the platform to begin my kilometer-long trek to the bus stop.

If it hadn't been for the earphones I stuck resolutely in my ear, the silence would have suffocated me. All around me stretched fields touched by nothing but the steel claws of ice, meeting at the horizon a sky so deep and black I felt I'd be sucked into it if I stared. I wore a headlamp to track my boots on the ice. The only other light came from the pinpricks of my neighbors' windows across the fields. Had someone told me a year before that this solitary figure lugging frozen feet across a glacier was me, I would have laughed.

The years prior to 2010 had found us half an hour outside of New York City. In the four years we lived there, my three older siblings and I inhabited different worlds.

Evan—who has since shed their binary gender—met friends through the ultimate frisbee team who would stick around to this day. The group adopted our garage as their home base, where my parents let them draw on the walls. Before we left Dobbs Ferry, Evan graduated high school and moved to Syracuse to study film.

Vera—second-born—entered ninth grade listening religiously to Nightwish and found herself in a class of textbook *Mean Girls* who flipped her off, unprompted, on her very first day. She bonded with less repugnant peers over all things horror. When she graduated at the end of our New York stint, she came with us to Denmark for the first half of her gap year.

Madigan, meanwhile, suffered through the worst stages of braces while changing crushes like socks. She exhibited her teenhood through drastic haircuts, outfits that now make her cringe, and an ardent dedication to learning Red Hot Chili Peppers' discography on the drums.

And I—baby of the family—finally outgrew crying every Sunday night when I graduated from Springhurst Elementary to Dobbs Ferry Middle School. It wasn't that I hated school; somehow, I wasn't friendless despite my teacher's pet status. Instead, my weekly outbursts were the product of perpetual movement. By age eight, I was living in my fourth country and starting my third school, and I'd accumulated homesickness like books.

My father's UN job meant we were used to relocating every few years, and we'd expected nothing else from New York. So far, the United Nations Development Program had shipped us from Vietnam to Mongolia to Almaty, Kazakhstan, after which we'd had a choice between two locations: Astana, the site of the UN's new Kazakh office, and the Big Apple. When we decided on New York I squealed, "People are going to speak the same language as us!" A foreign concept.

It was therefore a given that we'd leave New York as well, something I told my friends with confidence. Summer of 2010, I'd be out of here. We didn't even know where we were going. We just assumed we'd go somewhere, leave another home behind as we'd always done. We all agreed that it was time.

In the haze of that summer, when fireflies started appearing at dusk and sprinklers *chk-chk-chk*ed in neighboring yards, my friends threw me my first and only surprise party. They had scribbled messages all over a volleyball: *We're going to miss you so much, Jojo!* It made my twelve-year-old heart swell to the point of bursting.

In June we went to Bornholm, as we did every summer. On the ferry from Sweden we played card games, let the wind on the deck whip our hair into tangled mattes, and pinched the twenty-kroner coins our grandmother had given us all the way to the snack bar. Madigan and Vera argued over which licorice tasted the best; Evan and I agreed that they were all revolting and made a careful selection of chocolate.

On Bornholm we spent long, sun-soaked days pedaling our bikes to the beach, playing Kubb and Capture the Flag, and clearing brush across the property in our paint-stained work clothes. Madigan was the only one who got a tan. Evan and I alternated between sunburns and freckles, and Vera slathered her pale skin with sunscreen and armed herself with wide-brimmed hats. Because Mor vetoed Wi-Fi at our summerhouse, we entertained ourselves with other pastimes: books, yardwork, and old DVDs of our favorite movies.

But underneath the stretched, color-explosion sunsets that painted the sky mere hours before midnight, we were waiting. The UN was supposed to reassign my father to a new post, and we discussed the prospect of our potential home enthusiastically at first—Fiji? Belgium? Mongolia, for a second time? But weeks turned into months, and as we approached August there was no indication that my father would have a new country assignment by the time my sister and I were supposed to return to school.

I still don't fully understand what happened that summer, except that it had something to do with the internal politics and restructuring and red tape. What I do remember is an overwhelming sense of dread, shared by my family, at the thought of returning to New York. How mortifying, to have convinced everyone of my departure, to have been sent off with a surprise party and cards upon cards, to have said all my tear-streaked goodbyes—and then to crawl back into eighth grade as if I'd done it all for attention.

My parents listened. Understood our anxieties. Respected our wish to stay in Denmark until our future had something more concrete in store. Maybe if we knew we were approaching Bornholm's worst winter in forty years, we would have changed our minds.

Instead, my parents sat us down one breezy afternoon in July, pen and paper in hand, worry on their minds. Being twelve years old, I didn't know what they were thinking. I just remember something like guilt rippling from them like a mirage. They felt that they'd done something wrong. They regretted that things weren't going as planned, that we'd prepared to move for so long only to be left with this perpetual period of unknowing and a reluctance to return to New York.

That day, as a gust of flowery air billowed from open door to open window, we sat around the dining table and discussed logistics.

"So we've established," said my father, "that you four little darlings are staying here. What do you need to make this place livable?"

My dad's beard was darker then than it is now, though salt was already sprinkling his temples. He would look alien to me without a beard.

Madigan replied to his question without hesitation: "Internet." She was cooling to the idea of riding her bike five kilometers to the nearest library to get online. Mor, shaking her head with a smile, wrote it down.

"A washing machine," I said, thinking about having to scrub my clothes in ice-cold suds.

"A kitten," said my sister Vera with her usual sly smile. Madigan and I exclaimed our assent, leaping out of our seats when Mor wrote it demonstratively on her list. Not long afterwards, Sonja—that brown-black fluffball of a tabby—joined our veterans Smokey and Snowball, who by then had seen more of the world than most people and accepted their new friend in stride.

As August of that year rolled over us, thick with flies and harvests, my father flew back to New York where he would spend the year working, selling our house, and continuing to seek reassignment. He said goodbye with concern buried deep in his eyes. I didn't like the idea of him being in New York without us, riding the train into the dreary city and back. I didn't want him trudging into an echoing cavern of a house, no one there to answer his, "Honey, I'm home!"—a daily reference to one of his favorite movies, *Pleasantville.* I would miss waking up on Saturday mornings to his bottomless stack of crêpes, which thanks to him I pronounced "crapes" until well into my teens.

Much sooner than any of us would have preferred, Madigan and I enrolled in public school on that tiny island. I would attend Aaker Skole in Aakirkeby, the nearest town; Madigan, two years older, would take the bus into Rønne to attend tenth grade. Vera, meanwhile, would spend six months selling coffee and cigarettes to leathery tourists at a seaside café in Nexø. After that, she'd get on a plane to Beijing and spend the rest of her gap year there with a friend she'd had since our Mongolia years.

Until that point, my siblings and I had attended international schools dominated by the English language. We only spoke Danish with our mother and her family, patchworked with English words whose translation we didn't know. Several pages of my journal from that time are scribbled with misspelled practice introductions: *Mit navn er Johanna. Min mor er Dansker. Min far er Amerikaner.* I'm so grateful for Mor's persistence with our second language. How easy it would have been to give up, to justify concluding her efforts with the argument that everyone in Denmark speaks English, anyway. I'm bilingual thanks to her love of language, and her patience with children living the rest of their lives in their father tongue.

When I was six and we lived in the Kazakh mountains, I got lazy. "Mom!" I called down the staircase one crisp afternoon, no doubt to ask for her help finding something—which she always did within seconds no matter how long I'd been looking. She, at the end of her rope, replied, "My name is not *Mom!*" Then and there, she became Mor unconditionally. But it would take this year plus two more of Higher Level IB Danish to speak, read, and write more or less fluently.

Thus, I started eighth grade in Bornholm's sticky August heat with my Danish in disarray, a trembling mess of doubt and fear. My mother stood in the doorway with a furrowed brow as I prepared for the five-kilometer ride. I mounted my bicycle and blew her a kiss. Later, Mor would tell me that year made her feel ridiculous. The neighbors—ancient gossips with nothing better to talk about on an island where nothing happens—scrutinized us with expressions of silent judgment. What were we doing there? their pinched faces said. What were we thinking?

The sunrise blinded me on the first day of school, soaking the wheat fields in gold as I passed them. The Jersey cows up the road gazed after me, their jaws working away at mouthfuls of grass. Further along, three windmills that forever studded our horizon swung long arms—I could hear them swish to the rhythm of my bicycle pedals—as if waving me along, wishing me luck.

My only clear memory from that day at Aaker Skole was dismounting outside the low brick building and having no idea where to park my bike. Mor's voice echoed in my head: *Spørg bare hvis du ikke er sikker.* If you're not sure, just ask. So I did.

"*Undskyld,*" I said to two girls hanging around outside the school, both with stringy brown hair and wobbly wings of eyeliner above their lashes. "Do you know where I'm supposed to put this?"

I offered my sweetest smile to make up for Danish hung heavy with an American accent. They just stared. I blushed and turned away to figure it out for myself, wondering if everyone at this school would be quite so impolite.

Perhaps I wasn't as affected by their rudeness as I could have been, because no matter what ill will I met at school, Vera and Madigan would be waiting to hear all about it at home, poised to thrust abuses at anyone who wronged me. That year, my sisters and I became united in our communal in-between-ness—our out-of-place-ness, our in-the-dark-ness, our foreign-ness. Our genetic links were fortified through a shared love of horror movies paired with pizza and beauty masks, a strange urge to choreograph dance routines, and an inability to resist Blondie's *Greatest Hits* album—the latter two usually in combination. Even today, the opening notes of "Atomic" transport me to our creaky old living room, where we fell into fits of laughter as we invented mundane steps and believed ourselves to be brilliant.

I was accustomed to new countries and new schools, and if I'd developed one talent by age thirteen it was for making any place feel like home. Now, as I walked toward the bus stop under winter's pressing black sky, I looked forward to school.

Holiday festivity makes winter in Denmark bearable. In fact, at Aaker, Christmas seemed to be held to a higher regard than education. We spent a great deal of our December school days learning how to make paper stars and snowflakes, watching holiday movies, and listening to songs like "*Jul i Angora*" and "*Julebal*" and Wham!'s "*Last Christmas.*"

By then I'd made a few close friends. Therese and I bonded over her fascination with America, and our mutual schoolgirl obsession with boybands and—it pains me to admit—the hair-flip days of Justin Bieber. Signe and I, meanwhile, latched onto each other's shared introversion and love for the coziness that winter fostered. During one of my first weeks at Aaker, when our biology teacher asked us to group up for a project, Therese hurried over to me and said, *"Du skal bestemt være i vores gruppe, Johanna, hvis du har lyst."* Her inviting me to join their group stands out in my memory; her kindness was much-needed in that box of a classroom, where I felt I didn't belong.

I found the rest of my classmates either bizarre or intimidating. Because of our differences in schooling, I was two or three years younger than everyone else. The boys were several heads taller than me, their hair gelled into spikes so stiff they looked ready to draw blood. In keeping with Danish fashion, they wore skin-tight jeans and sweatshirts from H&M. Every single girl wore the same necklace: her name in cursive linked to a chain of silver or gold. They flashed at me from every angle. Mie. Nikoline. Pernille. Most of them weren't virgins, a fact that I—twelve years old among teenagers—found alarming. They all allocated strangely strict titles to their friends, going so far as to label them on Facebook. Each had a *Bedste Veninde* and a *Bedste Ven*: best friends, girl and boy.

I felt perpetually abashed in the presence of my classmates. Embarrassed by my fumbling Danish and overlapping teeth, by my adolescence and apprehension. They had known each other all their lives, as my New York friends had. But here, I felt that whatever charm I possessed was trapped in the confines of a language barrier. I didn't know how to be funny in Danish. My favorite class was English because everyone turned to me for help. I got an easy A.

I was therefore thankful to Signe and Therese for making an effort to be friends with the strange new girl. They made jovial fun of my Danish and taught me Bornholmsk slang. Signe guffawed when I referred to snowflakes as "snefnugger" instead of *snefnug*. My sisters and I took to calling our mother *skat* and *basse* and *mus*, the pet names that our peers called each other, and imitating their drawls. By the end of the year, I was well-versed in both Danish and strange colloquialisms that belonged to Bornholm's history of being yanked between Sweden and Denmark by kings. And I had made two friends so great I knew this year, too, would end with a tearful goodbye.

They made it easier to wake up at 5:30 in the morning for school. There we sat in the depths of December, the sky still dark outside, holiday comforts on the projector, as we sang along to Mariah Carey and fumbled over glittery strips of paper and counted down the days until Christmas Eve.

But on Christmas Eve, I sat in the living room with my head buried in an armful of pillows.

One side effect of moving to a new country every few years is that traditions become the most important thing in the world. The Stiefler Johnsons did holiday celebrations right, and every detail of our festivities live bright and shiny in my memory.

The year we lived on Bornholm, tension frosted the windows on the days leading up to the 24th. We'd been expecting my father a few days before, anticipation mounting among a flurry of iced sugar cookies and gingerbread, when a colossal storm hit. We were blanketed once again in snow, people stranded midway through their travels all over Denmark. My father called us from a gymnasium in Rønne, the seaport city, where hundreds of people were forced to postpone their Christmas celebrations to spend several nights in the presence of strangers.

We'd been buried in so much snow that even the ploughs were no match for it. Every flight to and from the island was cancelled. My father had travelled from Copenhagen's airport to Sweden by train and made it on the last ferry from the Ystad harbor to Bornholm. After that, there was no going anywhere. He even spent one night on the ferry, propped up with his hood over his eyes, as officials told everyone in Rønne to stay put. The next day, the ferry passengers were shuffled like quarantined prisoners to a school gym. It sounded like the beginning of an apocalyptic disaster. My father had abandoned his suitcases in Copenhagen, and he had no prospects of making it to our house until several days after the 25th. When we heard that, his voice issuing grainy from the tiny old Nokia, we all exchanged such distraught looks it was as if he'd announced he was divorcing my mother.

But, Dad exclaimed, they'd really made an effort. Ever the optimist. They—I don't know who—set up a sparkling tree and gave goodie bags to the children and played corny holiday music and served up a traditional dinner, gravy and all. There was even a Santa Claus.

This did not pacify us, cooped up in our living room fifteen kilometers away. December 24th of 2010 found us scattered all over the house in various positions of mourning. I sat in a living room armchair with my head buried in pillows in my lap, feeling colossally sorry for myself. I spent every year of my life looking forward to Christmas. It was only thing in my life that never changed. Without the loyalty of our holiday traditions, what did we have? A nomad family growing and changing and breaking up with each passing year. In my adolescent drama this delay, whose end was nowhere in sight, felt like too much to bear.

The rest of the family was in the same self-pitying boat. Vera sprawled herself across the couch. Madigan sulked in her bedroom. Our mother frowned at the dining table with her sewing. And the house was a swamp of woe-is-me until my mother thrust down her handiwork, leapt to her feet, and decided we *would* have a delicious holiday dinner even if it killed us. She began to allocate tasks to us all in the kitchen, doing the brunt of the work herself.

It became the year of three Christmases—or four, if you count my father's among strangers. The first found my sisters, mother, grandmother, and me at a glowing table of the food we'd just prepared. The familiar flavors of tradition managed to cheer us up that evening, as the Christmas tree twinkled its encouragement from a corner of the room. The second we celebrated several days later, when my father arrived with half the family's presents in his carry-on. He'd been among some of the first people to leave Rønne's lockdown, a caravan of cars following the snow plough that cut a narrow path across the island. The image of his arrival is clear as day in my head: us running into the courtyard to greet him as he tramped into the courtyard, dragging his suitcase across the sea of snow and gazing around as if he couldn't believe his eyes. Nose and cheeks bright pink in the cold: our very own Santa. And the third Christmas we celebrated sometime in January, when the snow had turned to ice and the rest of the presents arrived on our doorstep from Copenhagen.

My oldest sibling Evan arrived from Syracuse somewhere in the midst of all these Christmases, when Bornholm's little propeller planes started landing at the airport's single gate once more. We showed them around the white-frosted grounds. There was the enormous snow-woman we'd built in the backyard—arms long gray branches, a mane of dry yellow grass, throat wrapped in a scarf Madigan had knitted, eyes of stone. There was the mound of snow, so tall and thick that we could zoom down it on sleds or the puffy backs of our snowsuits. There were the icicles that spiked off the roof of the barn, meter-long swords that refused to melt. And there was the pond, a smooth plate of ice with shadows of algae frozen underneath.

It was truly the definition of *hygge: a quality of coziness and conviviality that engenders a feeling of contentment, regarded as a defining characteristic of Danish culture.* The house was warm with candles, crackling firewood, and the gas heater, whose purple heat licked the very corners of the living room. The Christmas tree glittered with string lights and ornaments I'd cherished since I was very young—porcelain angel with her smooth blue dress, wooden Santa in ice skates, metal bells etched with gold-threaded flowers, and the gold paper star at the very top that Evan had folded as a child. You could probably hear the laughter and the harmonizing hymns we sang every Christmas Eve, despite our lack of religion, all the way from Aakirkeby.

A stroke of pale silver had appeared on the horizon when I arrived at the bus stop. I was surrounded on all sides by snow-buried fields, the soil hibernating until spring flowers would be permitted to bloom. I looked forward to the day when I'd be able to shed my coat and gloves and bright red cheeks, when snowflakes would be replaced with humming honeybees. The roses would sprout bright green buds, and the apple and pear trees would be filled with papery blossoms.

My father would arrive, finally, with news of his new assignment: Abu Dhabi. It sounded deeply exotic. A metropolis in the desert, bordering the Arabian Gulf with its turquoise waves and hot, hot sand. Palm trees and streets misted with humidity. The kind of place whose extreme glamour only oil can bring.

For now, there was a mountain of shoveled snow by the bus stop, three times my height. I stood beside the road, watching headlights drift past as I waited for the bus to appear around the corner. I don't think a single bus arrived on time that year. How many hours did we wait in subzero winds, begging for the bus to turn the corner? How many times did it bypass us if we had foolishly sought shelter from the blizzards?

Even then, we talked about this as the year we would never forget. The year of the straw bale furnace, of sawing firewood in the woodshed, of Sonja's surprise kittens underneath the piano; of Christmas, tripled, and the Danish classmates we loved to imitate; of the uncertainty about our future, and how it created a bubble in which we could all feel comforted by one another; of mystery, merriment, and might.

The bus's square face of lights finally appeared around the corner, and I took off my headlamp to wave it down.

What do you do

Louise Watts

1st Prize, Southword Subscribers' Flash Fiction Competition

What do you do when you have bought your own home. What do you do when you have completed your therapy and you have a dog. What do you do when the gradations of the light are familiar, although still astonishing, and the shortening of the days brings with it the knowledge of all the longing from before, and you see that even longing is cyclical. What do you do when you suddenly, fiercely, with rage, want something you have not yet had. When you are driving from somewhere to somewhere and you see that it is soon to be too late. When your face is no longer what it was and you are becoming unrecognisable. When you have begun repeating your one poem and telling your father's jokes and laughing like your mother. When you sleep on a mattress on the floor next to the double bed. When you think you are almost at peace but then you feel your heart startle. If your heart were an animal it might be a dog and if it were a dog, you would be woken by the sound of your heart, as it defends itself and all that it imagines it has from darkness. When you wake in the night in the house that you own and you are lying on a mattress on the floor and can hear nothing but a dog below you barking and barking.

Last Kiss, Age 10

Nate Van Sweden

2nd Prize, Southword Subscribers' Flash Fiction Competition

AIDS was all the rage back then. Or at least it was in Mrs. Murphy's fourth grade class, 1983. There were countless ways that you could catch it. The world-weary fifth graders knew them all and passed this knowledge down to us. Of the myriad transmission routes, one was unanimously agreed upon by North Elementary's wisest.

"Spit mix," growled Steve, "It's an AIDS cocktail. Infection's immediate. No cure." He spat on the ground for effect. We all took a step back, afraid but grateful. Steve's father was a doctor.

*

Nikki floated into our lives from wherever new girls moved from. I loved her the only way I knew how—words sweaty, palms stuttering. Once, through some childhood miracle, we faced each other in darkness, huddled in a cedar closet at a friend's birthday party.
"I want to French kiss," she said softly. I froze—remembering Steve's spit-wisdom. I saw my funeral. My parents crying. Fifth graders shaking their heads in unison. As I leaned into the end, I said goodbye to my comic books. For a merchant of death, Nikki's tongue was surprisingly warm. She tasted like peppermint and probably hemlock.

*

Decades later I run into Nikki in a bar. In an awkward silence, I tell her about our AIDS near-miss. I scan the floor, suddenly embarrassed. Silence. She squeezes my wrist. Her eyes—warm, hinting a smile—raise mine from the floor. And—why not? I'd once given my life to kiss her.

Anchorite
Frances Gapper

3rd Prize, Southword Subscribers' Flash Fiction Competition

When I asked my friends if I could bring my anchor with its baked-on community of barnacles to their chosen restaurant they said no sorry it's getting a bit ridiculous you always lugging that rusty old anchor around is an unattractive habit amounting to a neurosis these days we never see you anchorless to which I replied unable to keep the hurt out of my voice well in that case I can't come either goodbye and I ended the call.

But they rang me back later from the twinkly terrace restaurant chorusing pleeease pleeease ok and the waiter led us to our two reserved seats usually waiters try to grab my anchor and stow it among the coats and my drunkenly apologetic friends toasted the anchor propped on its cushions one even kissed it leaving a lipstick mark and they refilled my glass and although still a bit tearful I started to relax and feel human and solid and like I belong here on this earth.

Ist Prize, Southword Subscribers' Poetry Competition

Taxidermy Heart

Lauren O'Donovan

When my dog dies,
I will cut beneath his chin and draw down
to his abdomen. I will open him, separating layers of fat
and fascia until I find cold viscera inside.

I will reach in, pluck out his heart to cradle
in my cupped hands the same way
I held his whole body to my chest the day we met.
I will strip his muscles, kiss each fibrous strand

that sped him across fields, through forest.
I will print his eyes in plastic—one iris bright blue,
the other half-eclipsed by a chestnut moon.
I will thoroughly flesh his hide,

removing every speck that gave him warmth.
I will turn out his lids, his lips, his ears,
and with a soft towel, absorb his last drops of slow blood.
I will apply a coat of canning salt on his hide laid flat,

wet side up. I will whisper all his names
as I rub the salt in circles.
I will roll his skin, hang it, dry it, tan it, stretch it.
Howl with it.

I will drape it on a cushioned mannikin,
pin it tight to his new body and lock stitch an invisible seam.
I will groom his fur, trim his ruff and tail, set his eyes, and then
I will curl him like a fox and settle him

on his bed in the living room,
one eye open in a slit, one ear half-cocked—as if
he has woken up just enough to notice me
and now will go back to sleep.

2nd Prize, Southword Subscribers' Poetry Competition

THE RAIN CAME IN TINY GUSTS

Christian Wethered

like flocks of birds
sparrows flying
the rain came in gusts
and the angry heart
this angry heart
was less angry
liked the sounds of birds
their feathery flapping
the black bark

and the angry heart
was less angry than before
now she was allowed to breathe
in silence
apart from the birds
the wind in the trees
their leaves waving
crimson and brown leaves

the angry heart breathed
as at the end of a long story
or a pause
slow cool breaths

she wished no ill of anyone
and by now there was no anger
anymore not a fleck of rage
not a crimson fleck
she continued to breathe
in silence
and the sparrows swarmed

she didn’t mind
she turned on her side and went to sleep
they swarmed
in the tree
quite a racket

3rd Prize, Southword Subscribers' Poetry Competition

Landings
Eoin Cahill

There is a moment just before the wheels of a plane hit the tarmac.
After you brace, plant your feet, sit up straight. Then, a stillness,
like a collective breath held. Newark, Alghero, John Lennon, Heathrow.

Newark. From there to Manhattan. Where I walk
the Sky Line, arrive at an alien structure rising out
of the ground. It's called the Vessel, a honeycomb like spiral of

one hundred and fifty-four interconnected
flights of stairs, two thousand five
hundred steps, eighty landings.

But it's closed, for a second time, maybe for good,
3 suicides in a year, reopened with safeguards:
a buddy system, extra staff, signs. Then

a 14-year-old boy jumped while with his family.
How Suicides At A Top New York Attraction
May Change What We'll Do For A View

"We are a little disappointed. We were looking
forward to the view" says a tourist, holding a
camera, surrounded by his wife and three kids.

When the architects and engineers sat down
to draw their models, did they look at the sketches
and think, let's lower your barriers here,

show more of that bronze skin, fabricated
copper shipped from Venice, for its mirror-like
surface, that will show every blemish.

When they test these structures, do they factor in
the loads that people carry up and down these steps?
Can they calculate the point at which that weight becomes

> the sum of all the pain they will leave behind,
\+ the fear of the fall,
\+ the pain of the landing.

When the billionaires and their
architects and engineers sit down,
they do not plan for ugliness.

And don't know how to speak with it. So they
shut it down. We are left with an object only
to be looked at, and a void at the centre.

Seán Ó Faoláin International Short Story Competition

1st Prize:

€2,000

Publication in *Southword*

Featured reading at the Cork International Short Story Festival
(with four-night hotel stay and full board)

2nd Prize:

€500

Publication in *Southword*

Four runners-up will be published in *Southword* and receive €300 (publication fee)

The competition is open to original, unpublished and unbroadcast short stories in the English language of 3,000 words or fewer. The story can be on any subject, in any style, by a writer of any nationality, living anywhere in the world. Translated work is not in the scope of this competition. There is an entrance fee of €19 per story.

Deadline: 31st July

Guidelines: www.munsterlit.ie

Fool for Poetry International Chapbook Competition

1st Prize: €1,000

2nd Prize: €500

Both receive chapbook publication and 25 complementary copies

Featured readings at the Cork International Poetry Festival
(with three-night hotel stay and full board)

This competition is open to new, emerging and established poets from any country. At least one of these winners will be the highest scoring manuscript entered by a debutant poet with no previously published solo collection (full-length or chapbook). Up to 25 other entrants will be publicly listed as "highly commended".

Manuscripts must be 16–24 pages in length, in the English language and the sole work of the entrant with no pastiches, translations or versions. The poems can be in verse or prose.

There is an entrance fee of €25 for each manuscript. Entrants may enter more than one manuscript. The winners will be selected by a panel of renowned poets.

The winning chapbooks will be published by Southword Editions and launched at the Cork International Poetry Festival. They will be for sale internationally through our own website, Amazon and select independent booksellers.

Deadline: 31st August

Guidelines: www.munsterlit.ie

Southword Editor's Poetry Award

€1,000 for the best entry of three poems

One entry only per person

Each entrant for their €24 entry fee will receive a complementary one-year, postage-free subscription to *Southword*

Poems will be read and judged anonymously by Patrick Cotter, current poetry editor of *Southword*

The winning poet will have their three poems published in *Southword*

If you are already a subscriber your subscription will be extended

Once a subscriber, there is the opportunity to enter, for free, other competitions which are for subscribers only

Deadline: 30th September

Guidelines: www.munsterlit.ie

the perfect gift for a poetry-lover
the poetry business
Digital Workshops
Recent tutors include: Romalyn Ante, Greta Stoddart, Jane Clarke and Andrew McMillan
the poetry business
Visit our website for more information on our **workshops**, plus our **writing competitions** and ***The North*** poetry magazine.
www.poetrybusiness.co.uk

Outsiders, Always
Mary O'Donnell
Southword 45
Queer Love

Contributors

Sallie Bingham's latest novel, *Taken by the Shawnee,* is a work of historical fiction, preceded by her memoir *Little Brother* and the biography, *The Silver Swan: In Search of Doris Duke.*

David Bleiman writes in English, Scots, Spanish and the reimagined dialect of Scots-Yiddish. Winner of Sangschaw Prize 2020 and McCash Prize 2023. Pamphlets available from poetrykilt.bigcartel.com

Dmitry Blizniuk is a poet from Ukraine. His most recent poems have appeared in *Rattle, The Cincinnati Review,* and many others. He is also the author of *The Red Forest* (Fowlpox Press).

Author of the 2023 Fool for Poetry Prize-winning chapbook *Levis Corner House* and Grolier Prize-winning collection *Some Far Country,* **Partridge Boswell** lives in Vermont and troubadours widely with the poetry/music group Los Lorcas.

Mattie Brennan's fiction has featured in *The Stinging Fly.* He has previously been shortlisted for awards including the Cúirt New Writing Prize. Originally from County Sligo, he now lives in County Clare.

Eoin Cahill is from Cork. His poems have recently appeared in *HOWL New Irish Writing, Southword* and *The Storms Journal.* In July 2023 he was a participant in The Stinging Fly Summer School. Find him @eoinspoems

Ryan Caidic is a Filipino creative director based in Germany. His poetry has been highly commended by *Poetry Wales* and shortlisted in the Peseroff Prize & Prism Pacific Poetry Prize.

Patrick Chapman's first collection, *Jazztown,* was published in 1991. His tenth, *The Following Year,* appears from Salmon Poetry in 2024.

Suzanne Cleary's recent books are *Beauty Mark* (2013) and *Crude Angel* (2018). Poems appear in *Best American Poetry, The Forward Book of Poetry 2022,* and *Poetry London.* www.suzanneclearypoet.com

Anne Connolly, once a finalist in BBC's Edinburgh Festival Slam, is a former Chair and Makar of Scotland's Federation of Writers. Anne believes Poetry is music in its own right.

Jack Cooper is a science communicator based in London. His debut pamphlet, *Break the Nose of Every Beautiful Thing* (Doomsday Press), received the Society of Authors' Eric Gregory Award.

Simon Costello's poems are published in *The Poetry Review, The Stinging Fly, Bath Magg, New England Review,* and *The London Magazine* among others. His chapbook *Saturn Devouring* is published by The Lifeboat Press.

Eamon Cunningham is a member of the writer's group in the Seamus Heaney Centre, Q.U.B. His poetry has appeared in *South,* C.A.P anthology *Threshold,* and online with *The Honest Ulsterman.*

Patrick Deeley is a poet, memoirist and children's writer from Loughrea. *Keepsake,* his eighth collection of poems with Dedalus Press, has just been published.

A resident of Dalkey, Co Dublin, **Katie Donovan** hails originally from a farm in Co Wexford. She has published six collections of poetry with Bloodaxe Books UK.

Ger Duffy's poems have appeared in *PN Review, Under the Radar, Poetry Ireland Review, The Stony Thursday Book* and *Wild Greens.* In 2024, she won the Desmond O'Grady Award.

Born in Belfast, **Rita Duffy**'s new series of paintings 'Persistent Illusion' opened at Crawford Gallery in Cork last year. Duffy's work is held in museums and private collections worldwide and her public art projects continue to grow in scale and ambition. Trinity awarded her the 2024 Charlotte Mexeke/Mary Robinson research chair at the University of the Western Cape.

Ruby Eastwood is a writer and filmmaker based in Dublin.

Mel Elberger earned an MFA from Brooklyn College and PhD from New York University. His recognitions include a Pablo Neruda Award and being longlisted by The Poetry Society (UK).

Mark Fiddes lives and works in the Middle East. His most recent collection is *Other Saints Are Available* (Live Canon).

Viviana Fiorentino's poems have been published in anthologies and magazines. In Italy she published a novel, two poetry collections and a book of translations. She is 2022 Irish Chair Of Poetry Student Prize winner.

Selected as a new writer for Cúirt, this is **Helen Flynn**'s first publication. A taste of her memoir, *CISEACH,* showcasing her caustic humour and brutally insightful reflection on a cruel life endured.

Frances Gapper's work has been published in four *Best Microfiction* anthologies, plus lit mags including *Splonk* and *Wigleaf*. She lives in the UK's Black Country.

Sergey Gerasimov lives in Kharkiv, Ukraine. He is a writer, poet, and translator of poetry. His book about the war in Ukraine, *Feuerpanorama*, in German, can be found on Amazon.

Alison Gorman is a poet and teacher who lives in Sydney. Her poetry has appeared in journals in Australia and in the UK. Her work was highly commended in the 2023 Mslexia Poetry Pamphlet competition.

Joanna Grant lives and works in the Middle East, where she teaches college classes to deployed American soldiers. Her most recent collection is *Adrift* from Alien Buddha Press.

Zoë Green is a Scottish poet who lives in Germany. Her debut pamphlet, *Shadow Child*, comes out this year; and her first collection with Valley Press in 2025. www.zoegreenpoet.com X: @thetrampoet

Katie Griffiths grew up in Ottawa. She came second in the UK's 2018 National Poetry Competition and is author of *The Attitudes* (Nine Arches Press) and *My Shrink is Pregnant* (Live Canon).

Tom Harvey's stories have been published in the US, England and Ireland. Tom is winner of the Seán Ó Faoláin International Short Story Competition and came second in the Mairtín Crawford award.

Lucy Holme is a PhD student at University College Cork. She was recently a finalist in The Brotherton Prize, The Mairtín Crawford Award and won the Cúirt New Writing Prize for Poetry 2024.

Mary-Jane Holmes is currently studying for a PhD in poetry and translation at Newcastle University. Her poetry collection *Heliotrope with Matches and Magnifying Glass* is published by Pindrop Press.

Julie Irigaray is a French Basque poet and the author of the poetry pamphlet *Whalers, Witches and Gauchos* (Nine Pens, 2021). Her poems appeared in *The Rialto, Ambit,* and *Magma.*

Johanna St John is a publishing MA candidate based in London. She discusses books on her YouTube channel, Johanna's Library. Swedish and American, she has mostly lived overseas.

Connor Johnston is an aspiring author who, like his favourite poet Gerard Manley Hopkins, believes that all poetry should be read out loud.

Maeve Keane is a writer and teacher from Cork. She writes for both children and adults, and was recently awarded the Betty and Jenny Bursary from Children's Books Ireland. www.maevekeane.com

Rosa Lane is author of four poetry collections: *Called Back* (forthcoming, Tupelo Press); *Chouteau's Chalk* (2019, UGA Poetry Prize); *Tiller North* (2016, Sixteen Rivers); *Roots and Reckonings* (chapbook). www.rosalane.com
Poem copyright note: The Poems of Emily Dickinson edited by Thomas H. Johnson, Cambridge, Mass.: The Belknap Press of Harvard University Press, Copyright © 1951, 1955 by the President and Fellows of Harvard College. Copyright © renewed 1979, 1983 by the President and Fellows of Harvard College. Copyright © 1914, 1918, 1919, 1924, 1929, 1930, 1932, 1935, 1937, 1942, by Martha Dickinson Bianchi. Copyright © 1952, 1957, 1958, 1963, 1965, by Mary L. Hampson. Used by permission. All rights reserved.

Eithne Lannon is a poet from Dublin. She has two collections published, *Earth Music* and *Everything Gathers Light*, the former was shortlisted for the 2020 Shine/Strong Award. www.eithnelannon.com

Mona Lynch has a master's in creative writing and is working on her first poetry collection. She has published in *Quarryman, Swerve, HOWL New Irish Writing, The Waxed Lemon, The Examiner, Park Poetry,* and *Voices from the Land.*

Niamh Mac Cabe writes poetry, fiction, nonfiction, and hybrid prose. She's published internationally in numerous journals including *Narrative Magazine, The Stinging Fly, Aesthetica, The London Magazine, Mslexia, The Offing,* and *The Irish Independent.*

Bernadette McCarthy's poems have appeared in journals including *Acumen, Agenda, Crannóg, The London Magazine, Poetry Ireland Review,* and *Southword*. Her chapbook *Bog Arabic* was published by Southword Editions (2018).

Kathleen McCracken is the author of eight collections of poetry, among them *Blue Light, Bay and College* and a bilingual English/Portuguese edition entitled *Double Self Portrait with Mirror: New and Selected Poems.*

Afric McGlinchey's memoir, *Tied to the Wind,* is forthcoming in Macedonian. Her two poetry collections were translated into Italian. A pamphlet, *The Throat-Bird* (SurVision) will be published in 2024.

Maeve McKenna lives in Sligo, Ireland. She is the author of two pamphlets, *A Dedication to Drowning* and *Body as a Home for this Darkness.*

From Belfast, **Paul McMahon**'s chapbook *Bourdon* was published by Southword Editions. Awards include The Keats-Shelley, Moth, Fingal, Plaza, Westival, Nottingham, and the Listowel WW Poetry Collection Prize. www.paul-mcmahon.com

Audrey Molloy's most recent collection is *The Blue Cocktail* (The Gallery Press / Pitt Street Poetry). She has an MA in Creative Writing from Manchester Metropolitan University.

Vicky Morris is a British/Welsh poet, tutor, editor and mentor. Her debut pamphlet *If All This Never Happened* was a winner of the Fool for Poetry International Chapbook Competition 2021. www.vickymorris.co.uk

Elisabeth Murawski's collections include *Heiress, Zorba's Daughter* (May Swenson Poetry Award), and *Still Life with Timex* (Robert Phillips Chapbook Prize). A native of Chicago, she lives in Alexandria, VA.

Damen O'Brien is a multi-award-winning Australian poet. His prizes include The Moth Poetry Prize, the Café Writers Competition and the Magma Judge's Prize. Damen's latest book is *Walking the Boundary.*

Emma O'Donoghue lives and works in Dublin.

In 2023, **Lauren O'Donovan** won the Patrick Kavanagh Poetry Award and the Cúirt New Writing Prize in Poetry. She is fortunate to have her work sometimes published.

Jamie O'Halloran's *Corona Connemara & Half a Crown* won 2nd place in the 2022 Fool for Poetry International Chapbook Competition. Her 5th chapbook launches this year. She lives in Connemara.

Ciarán O'Rourke's second collection, *Phantom Gang,* was longlisted for the Dylan Thomas Prize in 2023. His third collection is forthcoming from The Irish Pages Press.

Born in Romania (1983), **Marius Padurean** is half-hungarian, married with two kids, and moved to Denmark in 2010 where he has lived ever since. He is currently working on his second novel.

Gloria Sanders (she/her) is a poet and performer raised in London, of Spanish and Eastern-European Jewish heritage. www.gloriasanders.com

Mara Adamitz Scrupe is an environmental installation artist, filmmaker, poet, and essayist. She has authored eight award-winning poetry collections, and has received many international literary and visual arts awards.

Laura Jan Shore's poetry collections include *Breathworks* (Dangerously Poetic Press, 2002), *Water over Stone* (Interactive Press, 2011), *Afterglow* (Interactive Press, 2020) and *The Generosity of Birds* (Concrete Wolf Press, 2024). www.laurajanshore.com

Bobbie Sparrow recently published her debut poetry collection *The Weight of Blood* with Yaffle press. She lives in rural Galway, loves swimming in lakes and believes curiosity keeps her alive.

Former Santa Cruz county poet laureate **David Allen Sullivan**'s books include *Strong-Armed Angels, Every Seed of the Pomegranate,* a book of co-translation with Abbas Kadhim from the Arabic of Iraqi Adnan Al-Sayegh.

Nate Van Sweden lives in Cork. His work has appeared in *Ragaire, Swerve, Asylum Lake, Cellar Roots,* and elsewhere.

Csilla Toldy is a poet, novelist and translator. She makes film poems as a digital artist. www.csillatoldy.co.uk

Fiona Tracey is a West Virginian poet. She holds an MA with distinction from UCC, where she is pursuing her PhD. Her poems appear in *HOWL New Irish Writing, Stonecoast Review,* and elsewhere.

Louise Watts has published a novella-in-flash, *Something Lost.* She writes poetry and fiction. She won the 2024 Bridport Memoir Award and was highly commended in the 2022 Seán Ó Faoláin International Short Story Competition.

Christian Wethered (christianwethered.com) is a poet and songwriter based in Dublin. He has featured in *PIR, The Moth, Poetry Wales, PN Review* and *The London Magazine.*

J.S. Westbrook's poems have appeared in *Manchester Review, Magma,* and *New Criterion.* He currently serves as Assistant Professor of English at the Kazakhstan Institute for Management, Economics, and Strategic Research.

How to Submit

Southword welcomes unsolicited submissions of original work in fiction and poetry during the following open submission periods:

POETRY

What to submit:	Up to four poems in a single file
When to submit:	1st – 31st January
Payment:	*Southword* will pay €50 per poem

FICTION

What to submit:	One short story (no longer than 5,000 words)
When to submit:	1st – 28th February
Payment:	*Southword* will pay €300 for a short story

Submissions will be accepted through our Submittable portal online.

Our Submittable account limit means that we can only receive 1,000 submissions per month, so if we reach this limit before the end of January (for poetry) or February (for fiction), the submission link will automatically close and we won't be able to accept any further submissions.

If your work has been selected from an unsolicited submission and published in *Southword* before, we ask that you please don't submit for one year before submitting again – for example, if you were accepted in the last open submission period (2024) it means you need to skip this one (2025) and wait for the next (2026).

Visit munsterlit.ie/southword or southword.submittable.com for further guidelines.

Made in the USA
Las Vegas, NV
25 July 2024